"I don't want to go _____
I don't care if I never graduate! I'm
quitting!"

"You're out of your mind!" my father yells.
"What kind of a job do you expect to get
without a college education, let alone a high-
school diploma?"

My mother chimes in, "What kind of a man
will marry you with no education? You think
he is waiting out there to support you?"

"Don't worry about it. No guy has
ever checked my report card before asking
me out."

"If you quit school, I don't want you living
in this house anymore," my dad says. "Just
find out for yourself who is going to pay for
your clothes, records and makeup then!"

"I'll pay for them!" I shout.

I have $347.53 saved from Christmas,
birthdays and baby-sitting. That should be
enough for me to live on until I find a job.
I'll show them! I'll get some super job and
they'll see!

DROPOUT BLUES

Arlene Erlbach

CROSSWINDS

New York • Toronto
Sydney • Auckland
Manila

To my Husband, Herb

First publication March 1988

ISBN 0-373-98020-5

RL 5.1, IL age 11 and up

ARLENE ERLBACH lives in Chicago with her husband, son and two Siamese cats. A graduate of Kent State University with a major in Communications, she currently teaches a baby-sitting course for teens and is researching a book slated to be a guide to teenage boys.

Chapter One

"Chris Pattinos," Mrs. Bishop, my seventh-period teacher, snaps at me, "give me that lipstick! This is American History, not your boudoir. And there's a note for you from the principal's office."

While everybody stares and snickers, I walk up to the front of the classroom, wishing that I could temporarily self-destruct. The passionately-peach lip gloss is exchanged for the poison-pen letter.

Mrs. Bishop continues going over tomorrow's final. I try to act calm, cool and collected while I read over the pink slip of paper.

Chris Pattinos: See me after seventh period about final junior-year grades.
              Mr. Luella, Highland High Principal

It's not too serious this time. I'm relieved. I return to my seat, crumple the note into my purse and debate whether or not to bother seeing him. Not too many people know I have these meetings with the principal.

Most of my friends think I'm cute and bright. My image is a trick. It's like what they do with lights and mirrors in a rock video. The cute part I do with blue contact lenses, hot rollers and makeup. Or else I'd look like a desperate before in a makeover article. I need all the help I can get.

The bright part is the ultimate deception. I'm one of the people who make the upper half of the class possible, or I wouldn't have gotten the note. I'm sure Mr. Luella wants to discuss my almost perfect record for rotten grades. The reason I say almost perfect is I do well in English. My brain energy concentrates itself over that part of my mind and doesn't get distributed over the rest.

Mr. Luella and I have already had lots of talks. They started last year, after I tossed a bar of soap into a pot of boiling spinach during Home Economics class. The most recent one was after I squirted Mr. Reeves, the chemistry teacher, with a water pistol. It was an accident—one I got five weeks' detention for. There's not much Mr. Luella can do to me this time, though, even if I never show up.

My current term at the Highland High penitentiary is over the day after tomorrow, and in seventy-two hours I'll be experiencing the most sensational summer of my entire life. I'm leaving on Saturday for my job as a mother's helper at Devil's Lake.

All I'll have to do all day is take suntans, meet boys, watch Mrs. Kaufman's daughter, Glenda, and walk Geronimo, their Sheltie dog. I'll be escaping my nagging parents and Kathi, my pesky fourteen-year-old sister, plus I'm getting paid for it. I'll have a terrific time even if it rains every day.

Mrs. Bishop taps on her desk. "Don't forget about the Great Depression and World War II." She glances at me for a minute. At least she doesn't say anything to me about not paying attention. She was probably looking at somebody else.

School is so boring. Who needs it? Not me. I can't wait until I graduate and get a job like Mila, my cousin, who works for Lelane Perfume. Three companies were dying to have her, right out of school. She's got no homework, a new apartment and a car. I bet the job application didn't ask her why the stock market crashed on Black Friday. I haven't touched *America's Story* since the last final. As usual, I'll open the book tonight and squeak by with a passing grade.

Finally the bell rings. I flee from class and decide to forget the note. I need to get home right away and study for that history final. I have one in chemistry tomorrow, too. My mind is on so many things that I almost bump into Luigi Pasquelli.

Lou and I have known each other forever. It's not like we're madly in love or madly in like. We're just friends. Besides, he's one of the few people who knows about the real me, and he doesn't date girls who see the principal regularly. He likes girls who are pretty and smart.

Lou is Mr. Inconsistency. He wears black leather jackets and tight jeans, and drives a Harley to school, but he gets good grades in all his classes. He takes courses like electronics, business law and accounting. Looking at him you'd be amazed.

"Hey, Chris," he stops me. "What's happening? I just saw your folks in Mr. L.'s office."

"What?" Maybe he's been hallucinating. I doubt it. He doesn't drink or take drugs.

"I swear, I saw them both walk in. They waved to me."

"Trouble is right around the corner." Now I can't ditch the meeting, and it's sounding progressively worse.

"I'll see you later," he says.

"If I live till then." I feel like I've swallowed a snake and it's wrapping itself around my insides.

What if Mr. Luella tells my folks about the spinach and the squirt gun? I'm dead.

Unfortunately, Lou is not delusional. Perry and Terese Pattinos are right outside the office, and the vibes are super tense.

"Hello, dear," my mother says. She has the same look on her face that she had in fourth grade when my two pet turtles, Turt and Burt, died.

My father glares at me. He opens his mouth. My mother stops the profanities.

"Perry," she says to my father, "don't say a word until we all talk."

"All right," he answers. "But when we get out of here, I'm giving her a piece of my mind."

The principal ushers us into his office and shakes my parents' hands.

"How are you today, Christina?" he asks. I know he couldn't care less. High school principals do not care about the perpetually flunking. They are concerned with the brilliant, the talented and the jocks.

I want to answer, "horrendous." I smile and say, "fine."

Mr. Luella hands a folder with my name on it to my folks. He turns toward me. "Christina, we're all concerned about the poor grades you've had since you transferred here from St. Dominic's. You were a good student there. Is there some reason you're unable to concentrate here at Highland?"

I hear my father whisper something angrily in Greek to my mother. I hear words meaning boys and dating.

"Highland is a tough school," I answer for lack of anything better to say. "Maybe St. Dominic's didn't prepare me."

Mr. Luella looks perturbed. "I don't think so. Some of our top students come from St. Dominic's. Tess Horvath is a top student, and Luigi Pasquelli is working for the Youth Government Association this summer as a mayoral aide."

The Youth Government Association is big-deal stuff. Students petition, and are selected by town council to work as government aides in city hall the summer before their senior year. I applied to work on the Youth Government but I was zapped immediately because of my grades.

My parents look at me. Mr. Luella looks at me. I look at my fingernails and notice a chip in my polish. "Maybe my IQ is low. I'm not as smart as the other kids." I want to tell him I had a frontal lobotomy prior to transferring. I don't.

"No, Chris." Mr. Luella answers. "That's not the problem. I've talked to your teachers, and they feel you don't work diligently, except at the end of the semester. Then you get a good enough grade on the final to slide by. This year you won't be so lucky. There's no way you'll pass history or chemistry. You'll have to make up those grades in summer school."

"Summer school? I have a job out of town. I'm leaving Saturday. I can't tell Mrs. Kaufman I'm going to cancel at the last minute." I start crying.

"Chris, calm down," my mother says. The dead-turtle look appears on her face again. "After Mr.

Luella called, I notified Mrs. Kaufman that your sister, Kathi, is going to take your place.''

"You what?" I'm ready to commit murder. "Kathi is only fourteen. She's not responsible enough."

"Don't worry about Kathi," my father says angrily. "You worry about making up those grades, or you won't graduate with your class next year. No college will accept you."

"I don't want to go to college! I hate school! I don't care if I never graduate! I'm quitting!" I run out of Mr. Luella's office and down the hall.

My father follows me. "You're out of your mind! What kind of job do you expect to get without a college education, let alone a high school diploma? You're not qualified to do anything."

"Not everybody successful is a high school graduate. There's a girl in California who's a millionaire from making hand-painted T-shirts. She quit school when she was a senior. And there's a top reporter at the *Northside Journal* who started his career at sixteen. I just read about it yesterday." I love to go to the library and read bits and pieces about people. It's amazing what you can find out.

My father doesn't listen. He rants and raves. I'm surprised the hall monitor doesn't give him a demerit.

"As a matter of fact Mila didn't do so great in school, and she's doing fine without a college education," I tell him.

"I don't care about Mila. I care about you. I don't slave at my restaurant all day so you can quit school and be a nobody."

"And you," I tell him, "didn't go to college yourself."

"But I went to school to learn the language and take courses about business. I still take courses sometimes. I'm sorry I wasn't able to go to college. You should be happy we're able to afford it for you."

"What kind of man do you think you'll marry with no education?" my mother asks. "You think some rich man is waiting out there to support you?"

"Don't worry about it. No guy has ever checked my report card before going out with me."

We all perform the favorite family sport of screaming and arguing with each other. A few kids stop to watch us. Lou walks by and notices the commotion. I wish I could be transported immediately to another planet and leave my parents behind.

"I'll call you later," Lou says and walks away.

"I'm quitting and that's final!"

My folks and I walk to the parking lot, get into the car and continue arguing. They're incredible. A tornado could be whirling around us and they'd still be going on and on.

"If you quit school I don't want you living in my house anymore," my dad says. "Just see who's going to pay for your clothes, records and makeup then!"

"I'll pay for them," I tell him.

"Good. You go get a job and see how easy it is."

"Fine, I will. You wait and see."

"You try it," he answers. "You think you have such great skills?"

My father drops us off at home and heads back to work.

"Why do you upset your father like that?" my mother asks as we walk into the house.

"I'm not trying to upset him. He upset me. I didn't tell *him* to leave home, did I?"

I go into the kitchen and look up Mila's phone number at work.

"Chris, if only you'd try to apply yourself..."

"I'd get the Nobel Prize and find a cure for cancer. I hate school and I'm not setting foot in that place again. I'd rather not hang around here all summer anyway." I pick up the phone.

"You are being ridiculous."

"I am not. I'm leaving."

"I don't like your attitude, and this is going to kill your father." My mother shakes her finger at me.

"He's in good health." Guilt infliction is something my mother has developed to state-of-the-art.

"Chris, I'm warning you. You'll be sorry."

I ignore her and dial Mila's number. Someone answers, "United Pharmaceuticals." Lelane must be a subsidiary of United. I'm put on hold for a minute. I'll die if she ran off and eloped or something. Impossible. As of three days ago she had a crush on somebody who wasn't paying any attention to her.

"Chrissy, what's up?" She sounds surprised when she hears my voice.

"How would you like a roommate?"

"A roommate?"

"I need a place to live for a while. I'm sick of school and I quit. My dad is ready to kill me."

"Wow, your folks must be having baby dinosaurs." She's silent for a moment. "I could use somebody to share expenses with. When did you want to move in?"

"A.S.A.P. Like tonight. I'm dying to see your apartment."

"That soon, huh?"

I catch a note of dubiousness in her voice. "Are you sure it's okay?"

"Of course...you caught me by surprise."

"I'll try to be over tonight."

"I'll be waiting. The address is 2807 Fremont. It's near Loyola Avenue."

I hang up and start getting my stuff together. I'm not sure what to take since I'm not sure what kind of job I'm going to get. I throw in jeans, dresses and makeup. I can't imagine a job being a problem since Mila lives on the edge of Highland Township, near Chicago, where there's all kinds of work.

I pick up the phone to call Lou to find out if he can help me move. I hear my folks having an in-depth conversation, and I'm the focal point.

"Why did you tell her to leave home?" my mother yells.

"She was going away for the summer anyway."

"But she was going to be living with an adult and have her room and board paid for. Mila is only a child."

"Don't worry, our Chrissy won't make it. She's too spoiled and pampered. She'll be back home in a week. I remember I left home a few times when I was a kid and always came back."

My mouth is wide open. I'm seething. *You always had a ferocious temper,* I'm ready to add but don't. It would probably cause my father to rush home and give a full-fledged display of it.

I put down the phone carefully and go to my dresser for my bank book.

The balance is $347.53. My savings from Christmas, birthdays and baby-sitting. That should be enough to survive on until I find something. I'll get some super job and show them I can support myself.

A few minutes later, I hear my sister come home. She and my mother talk in the kitchen. I'm basically kind of nosy, especially if it concerns me. I try to listen to what they're saying through the vents. All I can catch is my mother saying something that sounds like Chris is going cuckoo.

Kathi comes up the stairs. I close my door. The creep walks right into my room and starts looking over the clothes I'm packing.

"Mommy says that you're running away from home." Kathi holds my aqua, vine-print T-shirt up to the mirror to see how it looks on her. It's my best top. One of the few things I have from Saks Fifth Avenue.

"Put my top down! I'm not running away from home, turd face. And I don't appreciate you grabbing my summer job!"

She throws the top at me.

"I didn't grab your dumb job. Mom set it up. You think I want to take care of Mrs. Kaufman's snotty kid and mangy mutt all summer? I'd rather take some extra courses and graduate early." She says the words "extra courses" loudly so Mom will hear all the way downstairs that her sweet, precious baby, Kathrina Alicia, is brilliant as well as unselfish.

"Sure you didn't want the job. You've been whining about it ever since Mrs. Kaufman hired me."

"I can't help it if you're a retard and have to go to summer school."

I slam the door in her face.

Precious baby screams bloody murder. My mother comes upstairs.

"Chris slammed the door in my face! I hope she never comes back. She's so rotten to me."

"Don't bother her," she says to Kathi angrily. "You don't want to take extra courses and you know it! You've been complaining about not having a job ever since Chris got hers. Be thankful Mrs. Kaufman was nice enough to hire you. She thought you might be too young."

I hear the two of them leave the house. Thank goodness! It's much easier to concentrate on packing without my mother and the head brat around.

The phone rings. It's Lou.

"What's going on with you?" he asks.

"Oh, a little family argument." I answer casually. "I've decided to quit school and move in with my cousin."

"What brought this on?"

"It wasn't sudden. I've been toying with the idea ever since I almost flunked biology last year. You know I'm no star student. My folks found out I had to make up history and chemistry in summer school and they gave my job with Mrs. Kaufman to Kathi. I've had it."

"Why don't you just make up the courses and go back to school in the fall?" Lou suggests.

"I wouldn't pass history or chemistry unless I got a brain transplant."

"So take something else instead of chemistry—General Science or something. C'mon, you can do it."

"But I still have to make up American History. It's a requirement." He's really irritating me. "Look. Quit bugging me. You sound like my mother."

"It's your life."

"Lou, would you mind taking me over to my cousin's place?"

"Sure. Where does she live?" He sounds exasperated.

"Near the city, by Loyola and Fremont. It's probably some fancy high rise on the lake, knowing Mila."

Lou answers, "It's near Loyola University. It's not on any lake."

It sounds even better. Lake or no lake, the place is probably crawling with college guys. So much for my mother's worries about what kind of males I'll be dating. Hah, I'll probably meet tons of college guys and I won't ever have to think about homework or tests again.

Chapter Two

Lou comes over a little later to pick me up in his Vega. The second he knocks I'm ready to split. I run down the stairs and go to the door. It's locked.

"Lou," I yell through the glass in the front door, "I better get my keys. My mother double locked the doors when she went out."

I go into my purse which is on the kitchen table, to get them. They're gone.

"What's keeping you?" Lou asks.

I motion my hands toward the back of the house. "I can't find my keys."

He stands by the kitchen window which he can easily hear me through. It's opened and we're conversing through the screen. I try to open the back and the side doors but they're double locked, too.

"Lou, you aren't going to believe this."

He looks up at me from beneath the window. "With you, anything is possible. What happened now?"

"My mother is making me a prisoner. I'm locked in! If this place caught on fire I could be dead. It shows you how much she cares about me."

"Do you have a door that goes from the basement to outside?" Lou asks.

"Lou, you are brilliant!"

I run down the stairs and unbolt the basement door that my mother has neglected to lock.

Lou is standing right by it. "You owe me one."

"Wow, I thought I'd never get out of this place."

After we barely stuff everything into his trunk, we go over to Mila's neighborhood to look for her apartment. I keep thinking of how exciting my life is going to be from now on.

"Are you positive she gave you the right address?" Lou asks. "I don't see any high rises here. I didn't think there were any around here in the first place. This is an older area."

Older is right. I wonder if I took down the address right. There's not a high rise or new building anywhere. The highest building is the Crossroads Hotel, and that's a few blocks away.

"Maybe it's a charming old brownstone, then," I tell him.

We get out of the car and start looking. Not only is the neighborhood devoid of high rises, most of the buildings are stores and restaurants. Lou and I get out of the car and start looking for the address. For a minute I think her address is a dirty bookstore. "Here it is." Lou points to a red building with a sign that reads Wilber's Choo-Choo Express.

"There must be a mistake. She can't be living in a restaurant. I'll go inside the restaurant and call her."

I notice a cute guy with auburn hair and a beard standing behind the counter.

"Where is the pay phone?"

He smiles for a moment, as if he knows me, and points to the back.

It takes her a few minutes to answer the phone. She sounds out of breath.

"There's some mix-up." I laugh. "Your address is the address of a restaurant."

"Oh," she says quickly. "I live above the restaurant. There are eight apartments above the Choo-Choo. I live in 3C . . . that's on the third floor."

"She lives above the diner." I try not to sound too disappointed when I tell Lou, who is waiting by the door for me.

"Are you sure this is what you want to do?" he asks.

Mila runs downstairs. She's wearing an expensive-looking, hot pink jogging suit and Nike jogging shoes, and her black hair is pushed off her face with a designer headband. She looks as if she's been exercising and still looks sensational. Mila always looks wonderful. After I exercise I look like something no self-respecting cat would drag out or in.

"It's up here," she says cheerfully. We all help unload my clothes, makeup, records and hair appliances.

At least the location prepared me, so I wouldn't faint from shock. It's a small living-room—dining-room combo, with a bedroom and tiny kitchen. It's not like I'm from a twenty-room mansion, but two and one-half rooms is a change from a three-bedroom house, especially since I expected a luxury apartment. And I can't stand chartreuse-flowered wallpaper or peeling paint.

"Put your stuff in the hall closet," she says. Lou helps me move everything upstairs. Both Mila's hall and bedroom closets are crammed with boxes and clothes. I squeeze everything inside the best I can. By the time we're done, the closets contain a conglomeration of designer everything, belonging to Mila, and my clothes from L. L. Bean and Discount Den.

Mila shows me how the lumpy sofa bed works, and by dinnertime, I'm situated.

"I'll take you all out for dinner," Mila offers. "Downstairs at the Choo-Choo."

"I've never been there," I tell her.

"It's very quaint. You might have noticed the display in the window; there's a train that goes round and round. The owner is only twenty-six. He inherited money from somewhere and bought the place. It's still pretty new."

The three of us trudge downstairs to the Choo-Choo. I notice a Help Wanted sign in the window.

"Perfect for you," Lou teases. "In case things don't work out."

"Yuch," I answer.

We all sit down at a table.

"Don't worry," Mila says. "I know all about getting a job. The best ones are in the Sunday paper or through Orendorf Employment. Don't do a thing until you go there first."

"I'll keep that in mind," I tell her. I don't want to worry about a job until Sunday anyway. I'm dying of hunger and I'm sure something fabulous will turn up.

The inside of the restaurant looks like a real train, with tables that have white tablecloths like in a dining car. Every so often a machine plays the sound of a train whistle. The place is kind of set up like my dad's restaurant. There are a few pinball machines and video games near the entrance. The front of the restaurant is a coffee shop where they serve light meals, soft drinks and sandwiches. The back area is where they serve heavier meals, wine and beer.

A waiter comes over to our table. He's the same guy I saw when I came in to use the pay phone.

"Mila, I didn't know you had a sister."

"She's not. Chris is my cousin. She's going to be my roommate."

"Glad to meet you," he answers. "My name is Roger Hadley."

I smile.

"Where are you from?" he asks me.

"North Highland," I answer.

"I didn't know such classy people would live above the Choo-Choo, unless you've just graduated."

"Not exactly," I answer.

Lou shoots me a look.

I ignore it.

"How about you?" I ask the waiter. He's very attractive and charismatic. There is something about him that makes him worldly, and it's not because he's a little older than the guys I usually date. I sure hope he's not the guy Mila likes.

"I go to Loyola. I work here part-time during the school year and full-time during the summer."

"What's your major?"

"Life." He grins.

"Me too," I tell him.

He hands us the menu. It's a huge three-page one. There's so much to choose from that it's hard to make up my mind. I decide on Number 16, the Conductor's Special—a bacon, lettuce and tomato sandwich.

Two guys wearing jackets that have Department of Sanitation written on them walk in and wave to Mila.

"You know them?" I ask.

"I go out with Ben sometimes." She points to a guy in his midtwenties. "I like older men, and he's with the health department."

"They collect trash," Lou corrects her.

The two guys sit down at a table next to us. A short man with slicked-back hair and a huge diamond ring talks to them for a moment. Roger brings them sandwiches and fries.

"Who's that guy with the ring?" I ask.

"That's Wilber, the owner. He's the guy I've been telling you about," Mila whispers.

Lou shoots me a perturbed look.

I never connected Wilber with the guy she mentioned a few days ago. My stomach is turning. It's not that I'm allergic to older men, but Wilber looks like an overstuffed game show host. I couldn't stand being near him, let alone kissing him. What is with Mila? I've got to hand it to her. He does look like he has the money that could keep Mila in designer inner, outer and underwear.

The waiter brings our food. "I guess I'll be seeing you often now that you'll be living upstairs."

"Sure." Then I notice something very odd. The sanitation twins walk out the back door without paying.

"Those guys walked out!" I tell him. Whenever somebody walks out without paying at my father's place, the person who waited on them gets stuck paying the check.

"Don't worry," Roger says, "they're friends of Wilber's."

After dinner Lou and I go for a walk.

"Looks like your cousin is very interesting."

"Do you want to go out with her?" I'd be kind of surprised, but by now I'm prepared for anything.

"She's hardly my type." He takes my hand for a minute. "Look, are you sure you're going to be okay?"

"I'm sure."

"If worse comes to worst, you can apply for that diner job."

"Thanks but no thanks."

"It might be good for what ails you."

"I told you not to bug me."

He gets into his Vega, peels off and is gone.

When I get in the door Mila tells me there's a message from my mother. I have second thoughts but I call her back anyway. The minute she starts talking, she's on my back. "You know you left the basement door opened. Anybody could have walked in."

"Then you shouldn't have double locked all the other doors," I tell her.

She starts yelling something unintelligible. I hang up. She calls back and starts up again.

I hear my father saying something like "she'll learn" in the background.

Then I take the phone off the hook and leave it off until the morning when I wake up.

By Sunday evening my mother has called nine times. She might as well make a recording of the discussion and play it back. Each time the conversation is identical.

"It's very lonely without you and Kathi around. Your father would love to hear from you." She makes it sound as if I've been gone for years.

"If he's so interested why doesn't he call me?"

"He's a proud man. Why don't you try to settle your differences? Then you can move back home."

"No," I answer, ready to hang up. I remember all too well our last argument and the phone conversation I listened in on.

Then she says I'm acting extreme and goes into a detailed statistical report of everything that can happen to a girl in the big city and warns me that unless I get a job, my money won't last.

If my parents offered me my own private phone number, a new wardrobe and a car, I wouldn't go back home, or even consider it.

Even though we're cramped and it's not exactly like I pictured it, I love living with Mila. I'm free from tests and homework forever; Kathi isn't here to aggravate me, and there's an interesting boy literally beneath my feet.

There's no "Chrissy where are you going?" or "Chrissy wash the dishes," or "Chrissy clean your room."

We haven't straightened the place up since I moved in on Thursday. Mila doesn't believe in cleaning up unless there's company, and I'm no longer company since I've paid two hundred seventy dollars, which is my half of the utilities and rent. There are unmade beds, dishes in the sink and clothes thrown all over the floor. It's what I call creative disorder. Of course, it's what most mothers would call a mess.

You have to be very careful of where you place things or they get mysteriously gobbled up. I've already lost my two rhinestone earrings and my Mickey Mouse barrettes. They'll probably turn up when we decide to clean, which will be whenever a male asks one of us out, but that's the least of my worries.

There is one minute detail my mother and I do agree on, which is how fast money goes in the big city. Between paying Mila and buying food, my nest egg has dwindled to $58.36. Everything in the Sunday paper is for people who are experienced, knowledgeable and well qualified. I'm experienced, qualified and knowledgeable about lots of things, except I don't see any jobs for someone who has expertise at writing phony absence excuses, making out, or sliding by on tests.

"Mila, it doesn't look like there's anything in here for me. What am I going to do?"

She turns down her *Exercise for Beauty* tape. "Why don't you go to Orendorf Employment? They've gotten every single one of my friends jobs, and it didn't cost them a cent. I'll take you there myself in the morning. It's on the way to work."

"How are you so sure it won't cost me anything?"

"Because most of the jobs are employer-fee paid."

"You said most, not all. What if I get one where I have to pay?"

"They take it out of your check after you start working. It's called the advance and deduct system."

"Great," I answer. "I can already envision a paycheck of one dollar and no extra change."

"They do it fairly. Don't worry. I know Mrs. Orendorf, the owner, personally. She'll love you. Show me what you're going to wear."

I go through my side of the hall closet and take out my aqua, vine-print T-shirt and its matching skirt. I had to go to five stores until I found a skirt in the exact shade of aqua. The black in the print top brings out my hair color, and the aqua brings out the color of my eyes. It makes me cringe to think that the head brat had the nerve to think I would ever consider lending the top to her.

Mila looks horrified. "You can't wear that!"

I check to make sure there's not a spot in the top or skirt. "What's wrong with this? It's my favorite outfit."

"It's not dressy enough for a job interview. You need a suit. You do have one, don't you?"

I show her my long denim skirt and matching jacket. Then search for my red, patch-print blouse— the one I got on sale last year at Neiman-Marcus.

Mila scrutinizes it. "That outfit is cute for school, but you can't wear it unless you're applying for a job at a square dance supply house."

She inspects my wardrobe. "You'll never get a decent job wearing this stuff. Your clothes are sooo unprofessional."

She goes to her side of the closet and takes out an expensive-looking beige linen suit and a white silk blouse with tiny tucks down the front. "This is what you wear for a job interview and for work. I'll let you borrow it for Mrs. Orendorf's tomorrow."

"Gee, thanks Mila." I try on the outfit. It makes me look very sophisticated. Actually, it makes me look too sophisticated. More like stodgy. I don't say anything. I'd wear anything short of cellophane paper if it got me decent employment. I'd hate to go home and prove that my father is right.

I take off the suit and get back into my jeans and camp shirt. "That outfit must have cost a mint."

"Two hundred dollars," Mila answers.

I'm ready to fall off my chair. For two hundred dollars I can get an entire season's wardrobe and more. "How could you afford it?" I ask.

"With credit cards. Once you start working you can get a credit card. If you pay it off on time you can get more credit cards." Mila opens her wallet and shows me an awesome collection of plastic. Some from the best stores in Highland and Chicago. "All you do is pay a little on the balance every month. Once you start working you can get a credit card and get rid of that tacky wardrobe of yours."

"I'll think it over after I'm hired." I'm more the cash-and-carry type.

"And tell them you're eighteen at the agency tomorrow, and that you've graduated from high school."

"Won't they find out?"

"Not at all. They love you if you have a nice appearance and do okay on their tests."

"Tests?" I thought I was through with tests forever, except for the kind in magazines that tell you if you are generous, neurotic, or what type of perfume you should wear.

"Don't worry, they're dumb office-practice tests." Mila studies me. "Maybe you should cut your hair. You'd look more businesslike."

"I like my hair the way it is." It's a little below my collar, and I'm letting it grow longer. Mila's is short and feathered on the sides and front.

"Sophisticated guys like shorter hair. By the way, what do you think of Wilber?"

I'm ready to throw up, but I say "he's adorable." I've learned from past experience never to say yech to anyone's boyfriend, even if he's an absolute scumbag. Come to think of it, Wilber is Mila's style. Her past boyfriends have been potential Wilber clones—the kind of guys that go to parochial school so they can wear a uniform. I like the jeans and khaki type.

I want to change the subject. "I like that Roger guy. What do you think of him?"

"He's cute but you'll never get much out of him. He's a college guy—established men can take you to better places."

"I guess." I go back to the paper and look over the want ads. I've got more to worry about than guys anyway. I've got to adjust to life in the big city, which may be coming to an end quickly if I don't get employment. Once I do get employment, it looks like I'll need tons of money for shoes and clothes.

It's total chaos when the alarm goes off at seven in the morning. Mila is running around looking for her red shoes, and I'm searching for the rhinestone earrings that I couldn't find yesterday. We practically bump into each other. The earrings are by her shoes. I go to the kitchen table, push away the dishes and check my hot rollers which are not doing a very good job of heating.

Mila is yelling in the bathroom. "The electricity is off."

"What are we going to do?"

"What am *I* going to do?" yells Mila. "My hair is sopping wet."

I start turning lights on and off. "We must have blown a fuse. What's the landlord's number?"

"Don't call him," she says shortly. "He isn't home in the morning."

We finish getting ready the best we can. Mila dries her hair with a towel and I let my hair go straight. I hope my chances for getting a job aren't ruined because my hair looks awful. I decide to wear it up with a tortoiseshell barrette, and forget the rhinestone earrings. Before we get ready to go downstairs, Mila takes two boxes out of the closet that have the words Lelane Cosmetics written on them.

"Could you help me carry one downstairs?" Mila asks.

"Sure." I take a box and walk downstairs. "How are we going to carry all this on the bus?"

"We're taking the car." Mila opens the trunk and we put our boxes in.

"Isn't it expensive to drive downtown?"

"No," Mila answers. "The company pays for parking. And I charge the gas. By the way—" she hands me a catalog "—if you decide to buy some new makeup, I can get Lelane products for you at a good price."

I look through a shiny catalog with the picture of a blond girl wearing a flowered dress. I learn that Lelane is the American product with the French touch and a price out of my budget.

"Look," Mila says as we near downtown. "I can't go with you to that interview. I have an errand to run. The agency is in that building at the corner. Don't forget to tell Mrs. Orendorf I sent you. Good luck." Mila stops the car and drops me off.

Mrs. Orendorf's office is on the tenth floor of the building. The door is locked because it's kind of early. I knock. A short, white-haired lady in a gray dress answers it. "Yes."

"My name is Chris Pattinos. My cousin Mila told me you might be able to get me a job?"

"Oh, yes, Mila. I got her a good job at United Pharmaceuticals. How's she doing?"

"Great. She's working in their Lelane Division."

"Lelane Division?" Mrs. Orendorf looks puzzled. "What kind of job were you looking for?"

I don't know what to tell her. There is something about this place that makes me uncomfortable. "I'd like a job like Mila's," I tell her. "One that leads to something."

She hands me a job application. "We'll have to test your skills first. Fill out the application and then I'll assess you. Don't forget to check off the office machines you've had experience with."

The application has about twenty-five different office machines listed on it. I only check two—the calculator and typewriter. I guess two out of twenty-five at age sixteen and one-half isn't that bad a record. Of course, I put eighteen on the application the way Mila had told me to do.

As soon as I'm done with the application, Mrs. Orendorf comes out with a stopwatch. I hate stopwatches. They remind me of Highland High School and their yearly standardized tests.

"These are your tests. We only send out our most qualified applicants." She looks at me. "Don't worry. They are simple math and spelling tests. The typing test is the most important one."

She gives me the English, math and filing tests. Actually they're pretty easy, even though that stopwatch is making me nervous. I'm sure I'm going to get placed somewhere terrific. She goes back into her office and shuts the door while she checks how well I punctuate, subtract, add and multiply. I hear her talking on the phone to somebody, but I can't hear what it's about. I hope she's not calling the school to find out how old I am, or worse, she could be calling my parents. They'll probably say I'm a mature twelve-year-old to make sure nobody hires me.

She returns with a smile on her face. "You did beautifully on the filing and punctuation test. You made three mistakes on the math." She puts a sheet of paper into the typewriter. "Are you familiar with the IBM Selectric?"

"Yes," I tell her. I'm too embarrassed to say I've never been near one. The one I use sometimes at home is an old manual. I had planned to take typing in school next year.

"Why don't you practice a few minutes and then we'll take the test."

The typewriter goes faster than my mind and fingers operate. It's really easy to make mistakes on it. I barely touch the keys and letters appear on the paper.

Mrs. Orendorf comes back into the room. "Now don't be nervous," she tells me. She sets the timer. "We'll give you a five-minute test."

I start typing slowly. I have this sinking feeling that my typing is not going to be fast enough. There are lots of long words, and my fingers get jittery. I swear this typewriter feels me sweating and is making mistakes to spite me. The timer rings. Mrs. Orendorf comes into the room, and I hope she'll offer to let me take the test over. She doesn't. She goes back into her room again. This time she doesn't come back with a smile. It's a look that tells me I won't be getting a job through Orendorf Employment.

"With all your mistakes you typed zero words per minute."

"Zero?"

"Well, actually below zero. You typed fifty words per minute with six mistakes. We count each mistake as ten words off."

"You what?"

"It takes about ten words' time to rectify a mistake, so that's how we calculate it.

"You should look for jobs that only require light typing, if any. I'll get in touch with you when we have something. Don't expect too much until fall, dear. There's a lot of competition for any kind of job, now with everyone graduating in June. Work on your skills, and tell Mila I'm sorry. She won't get her RFB this time."

"RFB?"

"It's our Referring Friends Bonus. Once we've placed an applicant we pay the referring person one hundred dollars, if the applicant stays on the job ninety days."

"I see," I answer.

"Mila must have forgotten to mention it."

I wonder what else she's forgotten to tell me.

I go to two more agencies. One only wants degreed people. The other gives me the same tests as

Mrs. Orendorf's. I get all the answers right on the tests the second time, but typing is what they really want. Most places would hire a gorilla in blue jeans if the gorilla could type well. I don't really like office work anyway. It reminds me of school.

I get on the bus, go home and decide to apply at the Choo-Choo. It would be killing two birds with one stone. I hope the job isn't already gone. I'll never make it as an office person. I hate to type.

Chapter Three

When I get to the Choo-Choo Express the sign is still in the window. A middle-aged waitress with teased black hair is waiting on, and flirting with, a man seated at a table near the doorway.

Roger is standing by the Pin Bot game. "I love you, I love you," he screams.

I'm dumbfounded. Nothing with guys ever happens that fast. Not with me anyway.

"Two hundred thirty thousand points. I beat it." He hugs the machine and notices me. "Hey, you look uptown today. I bet they hired you to be president of IBM."

"Not quite," I answer.

"You're sure good at that pinball game," I tell him. The highest anybody ever got on Pin Bot at my father's place is 210,000. I'm not crazy about pinball games myself.

"Not good enough. I'm going to play in a tournament one day. Wilber is real nice about letting me play on his machines. He's going to get more soon."

"Where's he going to put them?"

"In that back room, I guess."

Roger and I walk over to the counter, and he hands me a menu. I sit down on a red leather stool and skim the selections. My father's food list isn't quite so comprehensive. He serves mostly hamburgers, gyros and Italian cuisine.

Roger takes an order pad out of his apron pocket. "Can I get you something?" he asks.

"A Cherry Coke and steady employment. Is that job here still available?"

"As of two seconds ago it was. What kind of experience do you have waiting tables?"

My restaurant experience isn't a definite answer. My father hasn't really let me work in his restaurant that much, except when he's really been short of waitresses. I can't really answer yes or no. "I was practically born in a restaurant." It's not a yes and it doesn't qualify as a lie. Besides, what's the big deal about working in a restaurant? All I have to do is take orders, serve them, smile and collect tips. It's the type of work anybody can do. Even somebody who flunks history, chemistry and typing tests.

Roger bends down behind the counter and comes up with a legal pad. "We don't have any formal applications, so I'll just ask you some questions. Is that okay?"

"For sure."

"Name?"

"Chris Pattinos."

"I already know your address. What's your phone number?"

I know this is strictly business, but I like him asking for my phone number. "555-7594."

"Age?"

This is where the lies begin again. I know I should be honest, but I can't, especially after what Mila told me. It's like this other girl has invaded my body and is doing the talking for me. "Eighteen," I answer, "last fall." At least I'm truthful about the birthday. My birthday is in October.

"Education?"

"I just graduated from Highland High School." Once I start, the lying gets easier. I hope, if I get the job, that nobody I know comes in here and says anything to get me into hot water.

"Very unusual," he answers. I see him writing down some notes.

"I know it's unusual. Almost everybody from Highland goes to college, but I decided I wanted to do something else with my life. Something down to earth . . . until I ultimately find myself.''

I can see that Roger is not listening and I'm making a fool of myself. When I'm cornered I'm good at babbling on and on. If I utter one more word, I'm going to say something to get myself in deeper—I just know it. I don't say another word so I can stop while I'm ahead.

Roger looks at me for a second.

"Do you know Dan Horvath?"

"I know of him." He's Tess Horvath's older brother. I really don't know her too well, either. It's the type of relationship where you know somebody well enough to say hello to them, if they say hello to you first.

"He's one of the guys that rents a room in the house I live in. I guess he'll be back when the summer is over."

"That's nice." He's the last subject I want to discuss.

"Now," Roger asks, "can you tell a joke?"

"What," I start laughing. "A joke. How does that relate to the job?"

"We need somebody with a sense of humor, who can think quickly, like Ruth over there." He points to the middle-aged waitress I noticed when I walked in. She looks ridiculous in the short, red denim jumper and conductor's hat that she's wearing. I wouldn't be caught dead in that outfit.

She gives me a smile, walks over to her customer and writes something down quickly on her green pad. She tears the order off and sticks it onto a spindle in front of a window that goes into the kitchen. "Adam and Eve on a raft," she hollers to the cook.

"What," I ask Roger, "is Adam and Eve on a raft?"

"Two poached eggs on toast. You better learn that stuff. If you end up working here, you'll be on the breakfast shift. Now what about that joke?"

I'm stumped. It's hard to think of something on such short notice. I better, or I'll fail the Choo-Choo exam for being a waitress.

"Okay," I tell him. "It's dirty. I don't want to say it out loud."

He bends over and gives me his ear.

"A truckload of pigs fell into the mud."

"Ha Ha," he answers icily. "I knew you were an S.A.P."

"What's an S.A.P.?"

"A Suburban American Princess—young, sweet and naive."

"I am not an S.A.P," I tell him.

He ignores me and runs over to the end of the counter to wait on three people who have just walked in. The phone rings. He doesn't answer it.

Ruth is busy packing a big take-out order. "Somebody answer that thing. My hands are full," she tells Roger.

"I can't. I've got three heads over here and another takeout to get ready."

Two more people walk in and sit at Ruth's station.

The phone stops ringing, then starts again. I'm going to prove to Roger I'm not an S.A.P. and that I can do the job. I pick up the phone. "Choo-Choo Express."

"I'd like three cheeseburgers and a tuna sandwich on toast to go," the voice on the other end says. "And three Cokes. One with no ice."

"Who is it for?" I ask.

"Ferguson. Fred Ferguson."

I go behind the counter and yell, "Three cheeseburgers and a tuna on toast to travel." I go to the pop machine and start pouring the drinks into paper cups.

Roger meets up with me by the soda dispenser. "What do you think you are doing?"

"What does it look like I'm doing? I just gave the cook an order and now I'm getting these Cokes together for Fred Ferguson. Where do you keep the plastic lids for the take-out orders?"

I can see Roger stifling a laugh. He snaps a lid on each Coke for me. "Food orders have to be written down on the green checks before the cook can prepare them."

I grab one of his checks and write down three cheeseburgers and a tuna on toast. I stick my order on the spindle. "Now, do I have the job or don't I?"

"Okay, okay. I'm pretty sure Wilber will hire you. He really needs somebody for breakfast."

"Well, what are the hours. And what does it pay?"

"You have to be here at seven o'clock sharp and you're off at two-thirty. He pays three seventy-five an hour. That's more than usual, because you have to cashier in the morning besides wait on tables. You should make about forty dollars a day in tips."

"Wow, it sounds great." After work is over I'll have the whole day to myself, and I'll be making enough to get my own apartment soon. "When do I start?"

"Probably tomorrow, but you will have to get the final okay by Wilber."

"When will he be back?"

"You never know with him," Roger answers.

"I guess I'll see you in the morning then, or Wilber can call me as soon as he gets in." I pick my purse up off of the counter and leave.

"You're not leaving so soon." Roger stops me by putting his hand on my arm.

"I better show you around now because if he hires you you'll need to know what you're doing. There's only one waitress at breakfast until ten-thirty in the morning."

"Who's the other waitress?"

"There is no other one. There's only the morning girl. Our breakfast business isn't that big."

I know this will be a snap. Business was so slow when my father tried a breakfast shift that he canceled it. I'll do such a good job that Wilber will increase his business and pay me four seventy-five an hour before long.

Roger takes me to the area of the counter, near the sink, where Ruth is cleaning off ketchup bottles. He puts his hand on my shoulder. I'm tingling. "This is Chris. She came in about that job for the breakfast shift."

Ruth glances at me and puts down the rag she is using to wipe off the tops of the bottles. Then she takes the dirty ketchup lids and tosses them into some soapy water in the sink.

"Well, we sure need somebody," she says, "but you look kind of young for the job."

"I've had experience," I tell her.

"So did the last girl."

"What happened to her?"

"She quit."

"I am not a quitter." Not when it comes to jobs. School, of course, is a different story.

Ruth sees four people come in. She pours four cups of coffee and carries them, all at once, by balancing them on top of one another.

"Wow, she's really good at that."

"She's been in the business twenty-five years," Roger answers. "She's a pro."

"And that isn't the only way she's a pro." A short black man, wearing a visor hat and sunglasses, comes out of the kitchen. He's carrying a mop and a pail. "She's been divorced seven times as of last Friday."

Ruth hears him and gives him a wink.

The guy mops up the floor behind the counter.

"Who's that? The town gossip?" I whisper to Roger.

"That's Ned. He's our busboy and janitor. Before he started here, he didn't have a regular job. He was kind of an itinerant janitor, going from place to place to clean up."

Ned looks at him and scowls. "I was never an 'itinerant janitor.' I am a self-employed businessman." He mops up the floor and takes his pail down the stairs that look like they lead to the basement. "See you in the morning."

"Ned gets ruffled easily," Roger informs me.

"I think I've seen him before, somewhere," I tell Roger.

"He's weird," Roger answers.

Roger shows me how to pack my order and adds it up for me. When Mr. Ferguson comes in, Roger watches to make sure I count out the change correctly.

"By the way, when the sanitation man comes tomorrow, give him this envelope." Roger lifts the cash-register tray and shows me an envelope containing cash.

"What? I thought the township pays garbagemen."

"This Ben does extra good work so Wilber gives him a regular bonus."

"I thought restaurants had to hire private garbage collection services?" Maybe this part of Highland is different because it's so near the city.

"Let's not worry about the garbage," he answers quickly. "I've got to show you how to do the side work and set up for tomorrow. You're going to be doing the counter at lunch. You'll need to know how to make a milk shake. Do you know how?"

"Not exactly. The place I worked at before didn't have a soda fountain."

"Let me show you how to make a superior shake." He takes a metal mixing can out from under the milkshake machine. I can see that it has some milk and ice cream at the bottom of it, but Roger pours in more milk.

"Aren't you going to wash that thing?" I ask him.

"No, after we pour the customer his shake, we leave what's in and mix it into the next order."

"Gross," I answer.

"That's what I've always done, ever since I've been here. But I'll wash it out since you're so uptight. What flavor do you like?"

"Chocolate. Let's make a chocolate deluxe. With chocolate milk, chocolate ice cream and syrup."

"We can't do that."

"How come?"

"We use a special ice cream for the shakes." He opens one of the bins by the fountain and takes out a large cardboard drum.

"This is fountain mix." He gives me a taste.

"It tastes like vanilla ice milk."

"It mixes better and it's cheaper." He drops in two big scoops. "Now for some chocolate syrup." He presses the nozzle of the chocolate container and nothing comes out.

We're interrupted by customers. Roger goes under the counter and hands me a huge, plastic jar filled with chocolate syrup.

"Why don't you refill the chocolate while I wait on these people."

"Sure," I answer. That should be easy enough. It makes me feel confident that I'll get hired, since I'm almost working already. I hope Wilber comes in soon and sees how ambitious I am.

The syrup lid is stuck tightly onto the jar, and I can't get it to budge. I try to wrench it off with all my might. It opens, and the jolt causes syrup to splatter all over the front of my suit. My elbow hits the ketchup bottles, and they tumble to the floor with a splash and a clatter.

"Oh, no," I scream.

Roger and Ruth notice the commotion and rush over with rags. Roger wipes up the mess, and Ruth attempts to help me clean off the outfit.

The chocolate stains get worse and worse, and there is a big ketchup dribble on the linen suit skirt.

"I don't know if we're going to be able to salvage this suit," Ruth warns me.

"Maybe I can take it to a dry cleaner's."

"That kind of stuff doesn't come out so well. You don't know how many uniforms I've lost over the years to ketchup, mustard and chocolate syrup. Hope that suit isn't expensive."

I see Wilber walk in. He sees us. "What's going on here?" he asks.

My heart is pounding. Mila will kill me, and Wilber will never hire me now.

Chapter Four

"What is going on in here?" Wilber looks at us as if one dozen jars of imported caviar have been destroyed.

"Oh," Roger answers as if bending behind a counter cleaning up broken ketchup bottles is an everyday occurrence. "I knew we needed somebody for the breakfast shift and Chris came in. She's perfect. She even lives upstairs."

"Roger was showing her around behind the counter and the ketchup bottles got knocked over. It was an accident. I was cleaning them and should have known better," Ruth explains.

I'm too embarrassed to say anything. I'm probably the first girl in America who's ever been fired before being hired for a job.

Wilber looks at me doubtfully, but he doesn't start shouting. I take it as a positive sign of interest. "What restaurant experience do you have?"

I hadn't planned on telling him about my dad's place in case they ever run into each other. But I'm so scared now I know that I had better say something fast. "My dad owns Perry Pattinos Pizza Parlour on Ridge in Highland and the one in Rogers Park. I've worked at the Highland store ever since I was fourteen."

"They don't have a morning shift there, do they?"

"They did at the Highland store, but they canceled it. There wasn't enough business; the area is too residential."

"I need a real hopper for the breakfast shift. You have to wait tables and cashier in the morning."

"I'm sure I can do the job." I'm ready to tell him I'll work for free and take tips only.

"Okay, we'll try you," Wilber answers. "Roger, you want to come in mornings the rest of the week and show her the ropes?"

"Sure thing. I can always use the cash." Roger checks the floor to make sure there are no more pieces of glass.

"Terrific," Ruth says. "I hate coming in so early to fill in. I'd rather be a night girl." She waits on three customers who have walked in.

Wilber eyes my ketchup-and-chocolate-splotched suit disdainfully. "You'll need uniforms so you don't get your clothes dirty and a pair of comfortable shoes."

"I'll wear my white Reeboks." Not that I don't want to be dressed properly, but Ruth's shoes look strictly orthopedic, and I wouldn't be caught dead or alive in them. The uniform is bad enough.

"They have the uniforms at Greely's on Ninth and Central," Wilber goes on. "Just tell them you're from the Choo-Choo and they'll put them on my bill."

Maybe if I'm lucky they'll be out of stock for the next century. Wilber hands me two menus. "I want you to know these by Wednesday. You'll need to know the breakfast one by tomorrow."

"I promise I'll know every item by the crack of dawn." At least I hope I will.

"See you at seven." Roger smiles at me.

Whew, that was harder than I thought. Now my big worry is salvaging Mila's suit.

I go upstairs and change into green khaki shorts and a jungle-print camp shirt. Mr. Miracle Clean is nearby, and the ad claims "we can clean anything." I wonder if "anything" applies to a designer suit that wouldn't presently qualify for rummage sale reject status. While I'm waiting for Mr. Miracle Clean to answer, I leaf through a pile of bills that Mila has stuffed away in the yellow pages. The statements are right in front of me, and I can't help staring at an electric bill on the top.

It's a cutoff notice! I read it over carefully. It's printed on pink paper like the note from Mr. Luella. Maybe the standard shade of paper to print negative information on is light pink.

If bill is not paid by the above date your electrical power will be discontinued and a reinstatement fee of fifty dollars will be charged.

The lady from Mr. Miracle Clean answers. "Mr. Miracle Clean...Mr. Miracle Clean. Hello... Hello."

I'm so shocked by the notice I almost forget that I'm waiting for somebody to answer the phone.

"I have a linen suit with ketchup and chocolate on it. Can you clean it?"

"I need to see it first. I can't promise anything."

"I'll be over later. My name is Christina."

"Just ask for Linda." She hangs up.

When I get off the phone I examine the bill again. That's why Mila was in such a rush this morning. The "above date" was Friday. She must have paid the bill this morning—the electricity is on now. I figure up again what I'll be making at my job. It won't be long until I can get a place by myself; I certainly don't want to live with Mila forever.

After I take the suit to the cleaner's and buy my uniform, I stop at the Aphosdel Bookstore. Maybe I'll find a book on how to succeed once you drop out of high school. Or maybe I'll write a book on the topic myself. When I'm rich and famous the Highland High faculty can invite me back to speak.

The Aphosdel has lots of out-of-town papers. I look through them and wonder what it would be like to live somewhere exotic, which would be anyplace besides Highland. If I'd stayed in school, I could have gone to Quebec for our senior class trip. Then I notice a man who looks like Ned thumbing through a *New York Times*. I do a double take. Ned! He looks as if he can barely read the local newspaper, let alone the *Times*.

He picks up the *Times* and takes it over to the register. I follow him, but I can only see the back of his head. Now I'm not sure if it's Ned or not. The basic difference between this guy and Ned is that this guy is not wearing a hat or sunglasses. He's wearing khakis, a knit shirt and Nikes instead. In case it is him it doesn't hurt to be friendly.

"Ned?" I move toward him. The guy seems hurried and rushes out of the store. He quickly drives away in a beige Honda hatchback.

I can't imagine Ned driving a Honda unless it was one from 1960. Maybe he has a rich brother. Ned probably has to stretch his budget to ride the bus.

By the time I get to the apartment, Mila is home. "So how'd it go? My outfit bring you luck?"

"Yes and no." I'm trying to determine the proper moment to mention the suit catastrophe, without losing my present domicile. "I didn't type well enough for an office job, so I took that job at the diner."

Mila takes off the Ralph Lauren dress she's wearing, hangs it up in her closet and kicks off her Adolpho shoes. "Are you sure that's what you want to do?"

"Until something better turns up. It's good money...I think there's something I ought to tell you about your suit."

"My suit?"

"I got a few spots on it so I took it to the cleaner's."

"You what?" Her voice goes up a few octaves.

"When I was interviewing for the job at Wilber's I got it dirty."

"Are you kidding?"

I repeat the tale.

"How could you be so careless?"

"It was an accident. The cleaner's said they'd be able to take out the spots. Besides, I'd have gotten it cleaned for you anyway since I wore it."

"If for any reason that suit doesn't come out like new, I expect you to reimburse me." She looks through her closet. "What's new with Wilber? I wish he'd ask me out."

"Nothing yet. I only saw him for five minutes." I don't add isn't he a little old for you. *Little* would be putting it mildly.

"I think I'm going to start working on him soon." Mila takes out an orange-print jumpsuit. "Want to go to the Windy City Disco with me and some girls from work tonight?"

"You have to be twenty-one to get in there." With my luck the place would be raided and I'd get into big trouble. That happened to a girl I knew from school.

Mila takes a cigarette out of her Louis Vuitton handbag and puts it into a holder. "Do I look twenty-one or don't I? I can get you a fake ID if you need it."

"Thanks but no thanks. I have studying to do."

"Studying? I thought your book-cracking days were over."

"I need to know this menu by tomorrow morning." I glance at the entrées. "Let's see, a Crazy Omelette with toast and potatoes is $3.25." The bottom of the menu says No Substitutions.

"What's a Crazy Omelette?" Mila touches up her nail polish.

"An omelette with cheese, mushrooms, tomatoes and green peppers."

"Yuck," Mila answers. "You'd have to be crazy to order something like that for breakfast." She sprays some Eau de Cost-a-Lot on herself—probably a fragrance from Lelane.

"See you later," she says. "I'm going to meet the girls for a bite before we go dancing. You sure you don't want to join us?"

I shake my head no. "Menu 101 is this evening's priority."

Food price memorization isn't easy. I devise a system. I list the items on a sheet of paper starting with the lowest-priced items first. According to Mrs. Bishop, the gargoyle who flunked me, it's best to put dates in consecutive order when you're trying to study them for a test. I'm glad I listened to that piece of advice because it seems to apply to menu entrées.

A fresh egg and skirt steak platter is $6.50. It better be fresh for that price. Anyone would assume that it would be fresh, not stale anyhow. Whoever heard of serving rotten eggs.

While I'm memorizing the pancake and waffle orders, the phone rings. I hope it's not my mother. I don't want to go into a detailed description of my employment status.

It's Lou. "So how'd it go today?"

"Terrific." I fail to mention the employment agency fiasco. "I got that job at the diner."

"Congratulations!" he answers sarcastically.

"Don't be such a snob. Hunger is a basic human drive, and I will be helping to satisfy it. How are things at City Hall?"

"Great. Some of the kids on the project are writing articles for the *Youth Observer* about what they would do if they were mayor. I'd like to focus on various problems in Highland Township. Remember when I said you owe me one?"

I don't remember but answer yes anyway.

"Maybe you could help me write the article."

"Sure, I'd be glad to. Then you'll owe me one."

"As long as it's not illegal, immoral or expensive. Working on the project is almost like being a real politician. We have a mock political ball scheduled for the end of the summer at the Highland Country Club. They have me and this girl from Peabody figuring property tax bills on a computer. I'm not sure if I want to be an electrical engineer or an accountant now."

"Um-hmm." I'm reading the menu while talking to him. I'm still pretty pissed about the way he put down my position, so I'm not tuned into his summer employment monologue. "Did you know that pancakes with strawberries are sixty cents more than pancakes with peaches?"

"Chris, have you been listening to me?"

"Yes, but I'm studying now. Certain things are now an integral part of my existence since I'm in the real world. I'm no longer part of a world that does things in a mock fashion.''

"Sure thing, Chris. Have it your way and you'll be slinging grub at people when you're fifty. Not that there's anything wrong with it, but I think you could do a lot better. Why throw away opportunities?''

"Bye now,'' I tell him. I think over the conversation. I'll miss seeing him around next year at school. Next time I see him I'll apologize for being so mean. Now all I can think about is tomorrow and how I'm going to do on the job.

By six o'clock in the morning I'm not sure if I'm ready to jump out of bed or the window. I've already had daydreams and night dreams about what kinds of horrible things could happen this morning. What if twenty people descend on the Choo-Choo and demand their orders at once? Or what if I spill coffee on everybody? I try to think positively. After all, the worst I could do is get fired or appear to Roger to be a horrible klutz. I'm a nervous wreck, and the uniform makes me look like a farm girl wearing an outgrown dress.

I go down to the diner a little early. It's open. Ned has already started making coffee. I see him writing down something on a scratch pad, which he stuffs in his pocket the second he sees me.

"Good morning,'' I tell him.

He adjusts his sunglasses. "Welcome to your first ride on the Choo-Choo Express.''

I study him for a minute. He does resemble that guy in the bookstore. "Ned, by any chance were you at the Aphosdel Bookstore yesterday afternoon?"

"Of course not. Now what would I be doing at a place like that? Bookstores are for intellectuals."

"Do you by any chance have a brother?"

He pushes his broom toward the other side of the restaurant. "No. I have a sister. She lives in Vermont."

Roger comes out of the kitchen with a bowl of lemons and cuts them into wedges. The white shirt he's wearing behind the red denim apron makes me notice his slightly tanned skin.

"How are you today?" he asks.

"A little nervous," I answer.

"Don't be." He flashes that charismatic smile at me. "I can tell you'll do fine."

I'd like to believe him. One part of me thinks I'll do sensationally, and this other part is not quite sure.

Ben from the sanitation department walks in and sits down at the counter. "I'll have two donuts and two coffees to go. And there's an envelope in the register for me."

I pack up his order and hand him the envelope. Ben counts out two twenties and a ten.

"Thank Wilber for me."

I give Ben my sweetest smile as Ned watches the entire encounter intently. Roger is right. Ned is weird.

A few minutes later, a woman dressed in a brown dress and two men in business suits walk in together. They sit in a booth by the window. Not counting Ben on his garbage run and that take-out order from yesterday, these three people are the first real customers. I don't count the people I waited on at my dad's place—they were just to practice on, the way medical students use cadavers. I try to begin my career on a cheerful note.

"Good morning, I'm Chris Pattinos. This is my first day here and you are my first customers."

They don't seem amused.

The lady frowns. "Where's the menu?"

I hand it to her.

"Is that orange juice really fresh-squeezed?" she asks, as if she's the beverage delegate for the entire universe.

"Of course it is." I point to a big, white juice-squeezing machine. I take their orders and go make juice for them. While I'm squeezing away I notice Wilber's license on the wall. His name is Wilber Edgar Larsen. He's the sole owner. Then I take the juice to the table.

After sipping the juice, the lady stares at it so intently, I think she belongs to a religious cult that reveres oranges and meditates upon their juice.

"This orange juice has a seed in it," she snaps. "Take it back."

"I can't, you already drank some."

"I want the manager," she shrieks.

Roger hears us. "I'm the acting manager, the owner isn't here yet." He rushes over to the table. "Those are the chances you take with fresh-squeezed orange juice."

One of the men at the table does a quality control comparison. He stirs his spoon through it as if he's doing a scientific analysis. He informs the lady that his juice contains a seed and gulps it down anyway.

The lady gives both him and me a dirty look, but quietly drinks her juice.

Except for the orange juice fiasco, which results in a three-cent tip, the morning goes smoothly.

"You're doing terrific," Roger says when he sees me deposit my tips into the register and withdraw two five-dollar bills. "You'll do better at lunch. That's where the better money is. Too bad you're not old enough to serve liquor. You could make money at night with drinks. This place should be packed soon, now that Wilber has those pinball machines." Roger brings me a glass of iced tea.

Except for my aching feet, the work is fun. It's certainly a lot better than doing homework and worrying about midterms and finals. Plus I'm getting paid. I sit down on a stool at the counter to drink my tea. I only get one sip. A human invasion descends on the Choo-Choo. In about two seconds every seat in the place is filled. Each person is wearing a name tag shaped like a shovel with his name and Society of Asphalt Pavers printed on it.

Roger looks horrified.

"Roger, what's happening? I thought you weren't that busy at breakfast."

"Oh, I forgot to tell you," Ned says. "That big hotel restaurant down the way is closed for remodeling, and this is the closest place for breakfast."

Incredible. It's like one of my dreams came true. The kind of dream I classify as a nightmare.

"What do we do now?" I ask Roger.

"Take orders and serve."

Ned goes over to one side of the restaurant, Roger goes over to the other side and I take the counter. The place is so jammed that customers are standing by the counter waiting to be seated. I take orders as fast as I can. It's hard to write down everything quickly, yet neatly enough for the cook to read it. Everyone wants egg orders—some with bacon, some with sausage and some with ham. I stick all the orders on the spindle at once. A few people come in for takeouts. It's impossible to pack the takeouts, wait on people and cashier. I know something is going to go wrong any minute. It does.

"Who the hell made the coffee?" somebody grumps. "It tastes like rancid motor oil."

Roger runs over. "You didn't turn on the machine high enough and the water didn't go all the way through."

"I'm doing the best I can."

"Hey, girlie," somebody yells. "You over-charged me. Why did I get the Caboose Breakfast with ham instead of bacon?"

"Calm down. It's all from the same animal," I joke.

"Well there's a fifty-cents difference," the guy roars. I deduct the difference from the bill. He does not leave a tip.

There's more turmoil when a man who ordered a Crazy Omelette with no toast or potatoes complains about his bill.

"I can't have starch. I'm on the protein-and-water diet. I'm even cheating eating the tomatoes and green peppers. I expect a one dollar and fifty cent reduction."

"I don't think I can do that." I'm incredulous.

Ned overhears us and hurries over to the table. "Now, mister, you're a businessman. Is that correct?"

"Correct," the guy answers sharply.

"When you charge for a job, you charge everybody the same price regardless of the circumstances?"

"Yes, of course."

"Now, suppose somebody provided his own cement and tools. Would you lower the price?"

"No. I'd charge him the same," he says. "That's our policy. It's assumed that the customer uses our tools and materials."

"Well," Ned answers, "we assume you will eat the potatoes and toast when you order an omelette because we specify that's how it comes on the menu." He points to the No Substitutions blurb on the bottom of the menu. "We have our policies also."

Finally the asphalt pavers leave, and by ten-thirty I'm pooped. I feel as though I've been on a treadmill since seven. My feet are killing me, my mouth is aching from smiling and my Reeboks are no longer white. I pour myself another tea and sit down.

"What do you think you're doing?" Roger asks. He grabs a book and pushes it into a book bag.

"I'm sitting down and resting for a few minutes until lunch." I see Ruth and two other waitresses walk in.

"Oh no, you can't." Roger throws the bag over his shoulder. "It's time to start getting ready for the lunch shift."

"Don't you have people to help do that?" I notice Ned filling water glasses and placing them on a tray.

"Yes; you, Ned and the other waitresses."

Lunch is like the asphalt pavers but worse. Around twelve-thirty I take a peek at myself from the reflection on the pie case. I'm disgusted. The heat from the restaurant has melted my eye makeup, and my hair looks like black vermicelli. I think I better get a body wave A.S.A.P.

About two minutes later, Lou Pasquelli and some kids from the project walk in.

Chapter Five

Lou slides into a booth, grabs a menu from me and hands it to the girl who is sitting next to him. The guys sit across from them. "I thought we'd escape from the mundane world of politics, feed our faces and see you in action."

Now I'm really nervous. It's not bad waiting on people I don't know, but with my friends it's different. It's like being the only actor in a school play, and I'm the sort of person who is thrilled to be cast as a tree, dandelion or other background object.

I study Lou for a second—he doesn't look like the grubbily dressed Lou Pasquelli I've always known. He's not wearing his usual insignia T-shirt and washed-out jeans. He's wearing a freshly starched pink button-down shirt, khaki dress pants and a maroon tie. Everybody looks professional. For a moment I wish I weren't working here and had a slot on the project instead.

I place water glasses, napkins and silverware on the table. "What did you do to yourself?" I ask Lou. "This isn't the same Luigi Pasquelli who performs wheelies in the Highland High lot."

The two other guys laugh.

Lou pretends to polish his fingernails. "I'm cleaning up my act." He introduces me to the girl. "This is Anne Marie Bradley—from Peabody. She's working on the government project, too."

Anne Marie eyes me as if I'm a human oddity that has recently sprouted a third arm, which, incidentally, is something I could use.

"Oh, hi," I answer.

She smiles, takes a sip of water and wipes her mouth with her napkin.

Any prospective senior who lives in Highland Township is eligible for the project—not only Highland High students. Theoretically, you could attend boarding school in Antarctica and still be accepted for the project.

Peabody is a top snob private school, and Anne Marie Bradley looks like its walking ad. She's got a perfect blond pageboy, blue eyes and skin without pores. She probably doesn't need pores anyway, since she probably doesn't sweat even when she is playing field hockey. She's wearing a Liberty-print dress that probably cost over a hundred dollars and matching green leather shoes.

She takes in my red jean jumper. "I heard you quit school and live above this place." She forgets to add yuck, but I know that's what she's thinking.

"I'm an emancipated minor." I'm not sure what an emancipated minor is, but it's something I've heard of and sounds good. I had to offset her remark.

"Wow," one of the guys says. "You mean you're going to work here forever?"

"Not forever," I answer. "Until something better turns up."

"Like what?" Anne Marie asks.

"Oh, I don't know. I haven't thought about it. I better take your orders now."

Lou orders a skirt steak sandwich, fries and a chocolate soda. The other two guys order hamburgers.

Anne Marie looks over the menu. "I'll have chili and iced tea with three lemons."

"We don't serve chili after June first," I tell her.

"Oh, all right, I'll have an egg salad sandwich on white toast. And toast the bread lightly."

There are so many people walking into the restaurant, it seems as if half of Highland Township and the surrounding areas are famished in unison. A lady who could be a stand-in for the wicked witch in *The Wizard of Oz* complains for the second time that her soup isn't hot enough.

"This soup is ice-cold. Take it back again," she cackles. A woman with a howling baby asks me to warm her baby's bottle. This is all going on while Lou, Anne Marie and the guys are watching, and I wish I'd never been born.

I try to be as cheerful as possible. I take the soup to the cook. The cook has had it with me and her, since it's the third time I've returned the soup. "I'll fix her," he says angrily. He boils it until it's scalding.

I run the baby bottle under some water in the sink.

"This soup is too hot." The lady sputters when I take it back to her. "Get me an ice cube."

I take her the ice cube, and she's finally satisfied. She must have flunked manners in kindergarten, she has not uttered a simple please or thank you. I'm tempted to pour water on her and maybe she'll melt.

When I take the kids their orders, Lou hands me some yellow paper that he's jotted notes on. "About the article—I'm not sure what the biggest problems in Highland are. And that's what I want to write about. Since you're part of the real world, maybe you could help me with it tonight."

"I'll be glad to." I stick the papers into my pocket. My mind is so bombarded with the culinary interactions of Wilber's that I can barely think about anything interesting. It's as if my mind is numb and my IQ is slowly dwindling to zero.

Anne Marie gives a dirty look to somebody. I know I'm not acting paranoid if I think the look is directed toward me. I'm ready to say "We're only friends, you predatory female, and your folks would probably have conniptions if the butler allowed Lou into your house."

Anne Marie examines her sandwich to make sure there are no cockroaches or flies in it. "Doesn't it bother you that you won't go to graduation or your prom?"

"Not really." I've outgrown those things. Actually that's not what I've outgrown. What I've outgrown is the negative reinforcement I get from tests and all the rules you have to follow. I know I'll miss the good parts, like the dances and eating in the school cafeteria every day with my friends.

And I already own two gorgeous prom dresses. I found them at Second Editions last spring for ten dollars apiece. One is a red, strapless, full-length satin; the other is white taffeta with a black lace overlay. For a split second I feel that something very important is going to be missing from my life, or maybe I only feel bad because of my sore feet.

"Anyway," Anne Marie goes on, "I can see how it might be fun living on your own. I can't wait until I go away to school next year. I'm applying to Sophie Newcomb and Sweet Briar. I'm using Pine

Manor as my safety school." She directs everything to Lou, as if I were invisible. "There's nothing like a four-year party, with my parents paying for it all." She takes Lou's arm. "Where do you think you're going to school?"

"I'm going to the University of Illinois to major in electrical engineering. I've already sent my application in. My counselor says I'm a shoo-in; I can't afford any place too fancy. After paying for my two older brothers, my folks' budget is kind of colleged out."

"At least they're paying for it," one of the guys says. "I'm going to be footing part of the bill."

I guess I'll be saving my father thousands of dollars by not going to college. Now they can use my college fund to send Kathi to Harvard if they want.

"Hey!" Ruth practically bumps into me. Her arms are loaded with hot turkey sandwiches and roast beef dinners.

I step quickly out of her way to avoid a gravy-and-meat catastrophe.

"This isn't a high school reunion," Ruth says. "There're four ravenous people at the counter waiting for you."

I glance over there. Ned is already getting them set up.

"Looks like I better get back to work." I hand Lou the check. "See you tonight then."

"Make it about seven." Lou leaves two dollars.

The rest of the kids leave fifty cents apiece. I wonder if many more people I know are going to come in here. I'd love to avoid them if possible.

The rest of the lunch is a cacophony of moving chairs, clanging tableware and people chatting. Ruth also gives me some biographical notes. She quit school at sixteen to become an actress and married her first husband, who she divorced and then remarried three years ago. He's the one she just divorced. She's through with men forever. I've certainly felt that way a number of times. Just when I'm ready to take a break, she notifies me of a minor calamity.

"We're out of hamburger rolls." She looks at me as if somebody robbed the place. "I can't find Ned and we need supplies. That guy has a way of disappearing when you need something. They should call him Harry Houdini. Why don't you go down to the basement and get them. We need frozen french fries and napkins, too. We're running low, and my left leg is starting to hurt. You're lucky you're a young girl."

"Where do you keep that stuff? Roger neglected to give me the grand tour of the basement."

I follow her into the kitchen. She points to a stairway. "Just go down the stairs and turn right, there's a storeroom, cooler and freezer right by the stairs. It's right next to Wilber's office and the downstairs' john. And there's a locker room in case you ever need to get dressed here. But I don't imagine you would, living upstairs and all. The hamburger rolls are on the top shelf and those fries are in the freezer. And don't forget the napkins. You'll need to put them in the dispensers. Everybody has side jobs besides waiting the tables. Those are the rules.''

It sounds easier than what I've been doing, and I can't imagine getting lost in a basement, although any nearsighted mouse might. There are two open trash cans and a pile of paint rags and papers in one corner. I also notice a frayed wire near a ceiling that has a gaping hole in it. I better let Wilber know. He may be a slob, but I guess he's a nice slob and I certainly wouldn't want his place catching on fire, especially since I'm living above it. There's a light on in Wilber's office, and I hear voices. One sounds gravelly. The other sounds like Wilber's. Wilber must have come in through the basement entrance.

I knock on his door to tell him about the wire.

"Who's there?" he asks.

"Chris, the girl you hired yesterday."

He walks over to the door and opens it.

I see the man with the gravel voice. He's bald and wearing a dark green shirt and a light green suit. He's looking over a big blue notebook with ledger paper in it.

"What are you doing down here? Aren't you still serving lunch?" Wilber asks. He doesn't seem angry at all. He seems surprised.

"We needed supplies."

"Try to get them before lunch. Really, it's a lot easier for everybody that way." He closes the door completely.

I hear Gravel Voice talking low.

"Now stick with me and you'll save lots of money. You keep a set of books, I keep a set of books, and then there's one for the tax inspector. It's good to keep organized." He laughs. "I told you if you'd buy this joint it would be a gold mine. But you have to play your cards right."

I know I'm not supposed to be listening. I'm nosy, so I go into the bathroom, which has a slightly leaky toilet and a damp floor. The bathroom has an opening on the top, near a vent in Wilber's office. I stand on top of the toilet seat and listen to what is going on.

"Just give the inspector my card and fifty dollars and you'll have a hassle-free inspection," Gravel Voice tells Wilber.

So that's what's going on with Ben and the dirty milk-shake container.

"Hey, what's keeping you?" Ruth yells. She's standing at the top of the stairway. "You fall into the cooler?"

I flush the toilet for realistic sound effect. "I had to go to the bathroom."

I jump off the toilet, leave the bathroom and tiptoe back over to Wilber's office door to listen for a second.

"I'm sure if I clean up the basement, I'll pass," Wilber says.

"Don't worry. I'll have somebody take care of everything. They don't call me Swing-it Swenson for nothing. I bet if they reported every picayunish thing in every restaurant, the whole town would be closed up. Nobody would be able to eat out anymore. So when's the inspector coming?"

"I don't know. Somebody next week. They don't R.S.V.P. You know what I mean?" Wilber answers.

"Believe me. Don't sweat it," Gravel Voice answers.

I feel awful, as if somebody just told me that there's no Easter Bunny or Santa Claus. As soon as I get myself together I've got to find another place to work. If I can find somebody to hire me, which may not be so easy. Maybe I'll force myself to take a typing and shorthand course at night. The thought of it makes me ill.

I go to the cooler to retrieve the french fries. The cooler is really corroded with dirt. Then I take the buns and napkins from the top shelf of the storeroom. I notice a few fruit flies hovering over something sticky and a few minutes later I'm greeted by a gigantic brown mouse. My heart is beating so fast that I almost knock over three four-pound cans of Seltro tuna fish and a ten-pound can of peaches. I can't scream, because Wilber will hear me and think

I was fooling around down here or—worse yet—listening. I trip and drop everything. I hear somebody walking toward me.

It's Ned. Walking out of the locker room on the other side of Wilber's office. "That looks like a lot to carry. Need help?"

"Why don't you take the fries? You know Ruth was looking for you?"

"I had to change my apron. I spilled some turkey gravy on it." He takes the fries and buns, goes upstairs and places them by the soda fountain.

"Use the bathroom upstairs from now on. It's cleaner," Ruth says when I return. She takes the napkins from me. "And don't take so long when you're supposed to do a chore! You're worse than Ned."

"I better get back downstairs," Ned says. "The crowd has thinned, and I've got some cleanup to do." He gives me a wink.

Ruth hands me the tray that the pancake-syrup containers are sitting on. "Now you need to take the ones that are half-filled and pour them into each other so all the jars are filled. Fill the empty ones from that big jug underneath the counter. Then take a rag and wipe them off. And be careful you don't spill any. We don't need more mess here. This is one of your side jobs for the next two weeks. Then you'll rotate. I'm in charge of side jobs. It's important that the girls learn all that there is."

The job is really gross. I also have to do the same thing with the mustard jars, which are real sloppy and make a mess. I also have to wait on any people who sit at my station while doing this stuff. I wish I had two bodies: one to wait on tables and one to do the yucky stuff.

When I'm leaving, Wilber comes upstairs as though nothing had happened. "So how was your first day?"

"I made $52.47."

"Well, that's good. You're going to be a millionaire soon."

I see the clock strike two-thirty. I fly out of there as fast as I can.

The first thing I do is go to the drugstore and buy some Epsom salts to soak my feet in. I'm so exhausted I take a shower, wash my hair and conk out on the sofa. What a day!

The next thing I know, the buzzer is ringing. You'd think that Jack the Ripper was here to visit. Mila is screaming something about a boy being here and all she's got on is a bra and pants.

Chapter Six

Oh wow!" I'm wide awake now. "Calm down. He's here to see me. Just tell him to wait. It's my friend, Lou Pasquelli, from school."

I get out of bed and go over to the door. "Lou, you'll have to wait a sec."

"You knew I was coming over. You told me we'd work on this deal in the diner today."

"Okay, keep your pants on."

"It sounds like you're the one without the pants," I hear him say from the other side of the door.

I throw on a pair of jeans and a blouse I've picked up from the pile on the floor. Mila runs into her room.

"I'm really sorry," I tell Lou when I open the door. He's standing there with his foot against the wall and he's holding white paper boxes that smell like Chinese food. At this point the smell of food is sickening to me.

"I thought I'd bring in some romance of the Orient." He puts the boxes down on the table and takes in the apartment. "You know what, kid?"

"What?" I'm afraid he's going to say you live in a dump, but I know he'd never do that.

He surveys the room for a few seconds and doesn't say anything. The place is messy but Lou's house isn't exactly out of *House Beautiful*. Both his parents work long hours. His dad is a plumber, and his mom is a nurse.

"You are really spaced," he finally answers.

"I'm sorry. I was exhausted after all that work today. It wore me out. You ought to know. Your mom's on her feet all day."

"But she gets paid about sixteen dollars an hour for it and she's helping humanity." Lou is very proud of his mother. She got married at seventeen, became a nurse and raised three children. She's been at the same hospital for years. Lou sits down at the table and opens chop suey and egg rolls. I get two mismatched plates and some silverware out of the cupboard. I hand Lou the least-chipped plate. Lou dumps some chop suey onto each plate and lays into it ravenously with a slightly bent fork.

Mila comes out of her room wearing an extremely low-cut, black piqué sundress and big, white button earrings with black speckles on them. Her shoes are black-and-white leather, too.

"Want some egg roll?" I ask her.

"No, I thought I'd leave you two alone and go scout the male animal." She sprays perfume on herself, examines herself in her compact mirror and goes out the door.

"Now for the fortune cookies," Lou says as we finish. He hands me a crisp brown triangle.

I crack it open and read the slip of paper. "'You will find exciting discoveries.'"

Lou opens his. "'Riches and love await you.' Maybe I'll buy a lottery ticket," he muses. "Do you still have that paper I gave you?" I get out my uniform and fish the papers out of my pocket. They're wrinkled but I can still read them. Lou's list is very comprehensive.

If I were mayor I'd:
    Get rid of graffiti
    Get rid of gangs
    Improve race relations
    Gain revenue through street fairs
    Conquer crime
    Feed the homeless
    Improve parking conditions
    Start neighborhood rehab programs

"Lou, these ideas are great, but you can't put this in one *Youth Observer* article, unless they're planning a series. You need to have a focus. I think I have a dynamite idea that a prospective mayor should be involved in that nobody else would think of."

"What?"

"Corruption!"

"Corruption? Why would I want to write about that?"

"Because I think I'm onto something?"

"Onto what?" Lou looks at me as if I'm crazy.

"I think Wilber is paying off people to cover his violations of health department rules and other stuff. He was talking to this guy called Swing-it Swenson today in the basement...."

Lou puts his foot on the wall, crosses his arms in front of him and gives me a cold stare. "If this guy was doing all this stuff, do you think he'd be talking about it in front of you?"

"He wasn't talking about it in front of me. More like behind me or beside me. I was downstairs standing on the toilet next to his office and overheard everything."

Lou puts his hand on my head as if I have a fever. "Either you're delirious or you've seen too many movies."

"I have not! Remember that garbageman Mila was dating?"

"Oh yes, Mr. Sanitation himself." Lou is beginning to show a spark of interest.

"I gave him a fifty-dollar bonus today for picking up garbage. According to my father, you have to hire a separate dumpster company if you're a business. You can't hire a city worker. It's against the law."

"He's hardly committing grand larceny," Lou answers. "You can't throw him in the slammer for that. A fine or slap on the hand sounds more appropriate."

"But there's more. That Swenson guy said to have three separate sets of books, one for Wilber, one for the IRS and one for the accountant."

"Sounds like creative accounting, if you ask me." Lou is looking more interested.

"And I need you to do a favor for me."

"I hate to find out what." Lou takes the Chinese food containers and throws them in the trash.

"You know the black guy with the sunglasses that was cleaning up the counter? He's weird."

"I heartily agree. Anybody who wears a hat and sunglasses inside in the middle of June is loony-tunes."

"It's not that kind of weird. He looks as though he's one step out off the street, yet he's really pretty bright."

"What do you want me to do? Get him an appointment for vocational counseling? Maybe you two could go together."

"I want you to follow him home."

Lou sits on the sofa and grimaces as if I had asked him to junk his Harley.

"You must be out of your mind! A guy like that probably lives someplace where I'd get jumped. Chris, look, we've been friends a long time. Ever since you let me use your gold crayon in kindergarten, but I'm not following some borderline derelict home for you. Why don't you use that pretty and smart head of yours and go back to school. If you'd forget playing waitress and Nosy Parker Pattinos you'd probably be the class valedictorian."

It's not that I'm too lazy to follow Ned. I'm afraid he'll notice me. I try to persuade Lou in a way that will appeal to his masculinity and make him stop the lecture. "Then I guess I'll follow Ned home myself. If I'm jumped and become a front page news item you can remember me. I'd like red and yellow tulips on my grave."

"Okay, okay. Friday we get off early. I'll follow him. If the neighborhood gets too raunchy, I'll head home. Deal?"

We shake hands on it. "Now, about the article. Do you think you could have something ready for me by Saturday? Some of the kids are going to the beach. Why don't you join us and bring it then?"

"I'd love to. What time?"

"In the morning, about ten or so. I want to be there and catch the best rays." Lou smoothes his hair and snaps his fingers.

"That's too early. I have to work."

"Oh well, maybe you can go another time."

I'm kind of disappointed now. Right after Mrs. Kaufman hired me I bought a gorgeous turquoise-print bikini and matching cover-up. I hope I get to wear it this summer, and I'd love to wear it in front of Anne Marie. She doesn't have as much of a figure as I do. Unlike Mila, the beach is the only place I've got the nerve to show my body off.

"How many days are you working anyway? I don't want this Wilber to be abusing the child labor laws with my friends."

"Six days, and in spite of everything it's real good money. I'm making almost four hundred dollars a week."

He stares at me blankly. "Money isn't everything."

"Does Anne Marie feel that way?" Anne Marie probably walks on the other side of the street when she passes Discount Den.

"What does Anne Marie have to do with it?" He gets red. "I bet you're jealous."

"I am not. I wouldn't care if you dated Brooke Shields or a two-headed porpoise."

"Okay, okay, so she is kind of interesting. I never met anybody so upper crust before. Once you get out in the world you get a chance to meet people from different backgrounds."

"I'll say that again. Are you taking Anne Marie to the mock ball? It wouldn't be a novelty to her, though, she probably started going there in utero."

He walks toward the door. "Maybe. I've never been there before. I'm going to rent a black tux for the occasion."

"Are you planning on joining the country club, too?" I joke.

"For sure. They're going to knock on my father's van that says Call Iggy Pasquelli for Service, and track my ma down at the intensive care unit of Holy Cross Hospital to see if they want to be members. But maybe when I've got my own engineering or accounting firm, I'll join. I'll invite you there in your waitress uniform. Maybe I'll have enough clout to hire you."

"Very funny."

"By the way, what's the full name of the guy who runs that place downstairs?"

"Wilber Edgar Larsen."

He gives me an evil laugh and runs down the stairs. I watch out the window as he gets onto his Harley. He sees me, tips his helmet at me and waves.

Except for a few mixed-up orders and stiffs— people who walked out without paying—things don't go too badly the first week. By Friday I'm as professional as Ruth, with foot blisters and scalded fingers to prove it, as well as two hundred and seventy-five dollars in tips richer. I've also managed to dodge the people who come in here that know me. I've noticed that the Choo-Choo's pinball machines are missing their city licenses and the bartender isn't too persnickety about who gets served. Roger is pretty friendly to me, but I can't tell if he's ever going to ask me anywhere.

Finally, on Friday morning, he puts his arm around me while I'm removing French toast residue from a table. "What are you doing tomorrow night?"

I'm thrilled, but hate to sound desperate. Especially with somebody like Roger. "Well, I had some plans, but they fell through."

"Great. The guys at my place are having a house-party. You want to come?"

Pride is overtaking me. I realize this isn't exactly a date but I want to go anyhow. "Uh, where do you live?"

"I live at 3705 North Roscoe, near Janson and Roscoe."

My heart drops down to my belly button. Janson and Roscoe is across the Highland border near an area called the Jungle. It's a conglomeration of old houses and abandoned factories. It's the sort of area that breeds rumors and lurid news stories.

"I'm not familiar with that neighborhood," I tell him. "I know where it is, but I've never been there."

"I'll be happy to come get you. As long as I'll be coming back to this neighborhood, I'd like to stop at The Greasy Grind."

"You want to what?"

"To shoot a few games of pinball. Greasy's is a great pinball parlor. Maybe I'll show you some of the ropes."

"Sure thing," I answer. I'm feeling more dubious about our relationship. I've never been to The Greasy Grind Pinball Emporium, but somehow it doesn't sound like the location for a first date.

"And by the way." He fishes something out of his pocket and hands it to me. It's three keys on a metal ring.

"What's this?"

"Your Choo-Choo graduation present. You'll need these to get in each morning. Wilber thinks you're doing great. So I won't be coming in mornings anymore. See you tomorrow at seven."

"Thanks." I put the keys in my pocket. I don't know if I'm happy or sad. I'm kind of disappointed. I was hoping for a regular date, but I guess you can't always have everything. I have proven to myself that a college hunk would ask me out without me having a high school education. And I am doing a good job, except I'm not as happy about everything as I'd thought I'd be. I'd like to discuss it with Mila, but she's not that kind of person, and she's really late this evening getting home.

"Where have you been?" I ask her when she walks in the door. She looks dejected.

"I stopped at the Choo-Choo to see how things were with Wilber." She frowns. "He is about the most unresponsive male I've ever dealt with."

I neglect to say anything about him. Like maybe he's involved with the Swedish Mafia. I realize my imagination could be running away with me, but he is the last person I'd want to go out with.

Mila flops on the sofa and stares at one of her fashion magazines. "Maybe I should wear different clothes."

"I don't know," I answer.

The phone rings. Mila grabs it, then hands it to me with a look of disappointment.

"It's Lou."

"I followed that guy," he tells me.

"And what happened?"

"He went through that big park by Mundelein and Howard."

"The one where the bag ladies congregate?"

"Yeah, and get this. He gave a big bag of rolls to one of the ladies."

"What? Are you joking?"

"And then he went through to the Mundelein side where those high rises are, off the lake."

"Those high rises are expensive. Which one did he go into?"

"I think that pink brick...no, maybe it was the glass one. I don't know, Chris. As soon as he crossed the street a couple of buses and a truck went by."

"Do you think...? He couldn't possibly live there."

"I think he works there. That's what I think. Maybe he's a night watchman or doorman. But I did find out something sort of strange though."

"What?"

"I looked up Wilber's in the tax bills and there's no Wilber's, no Choo-Choo Express and no Wilber Larsen listed at all."

"Are you serious?"

"Well, it didn't come up on the computer. Maybe it's because he's new. Maybe that's the reason."

"I'll be able to find out more about it tomorrow."

"Tomorrow, huh?"

"I'm going out with that Roger from the restaurant."

"So you're killing a few birds with one stone. Ya know, you should never mix business with pleasure."

"So what if I am? Is Anne Marie going swimming with you tomorrow?"

"Sure she is," he answers.

"Have a pleasant swim."

Chapter Seven

Mila and I are busy cleaning up the apartment since we are both being picked up by dates. Cleaning up means hanging up our clothes, washing dishes and pushing magazines and dirty laundry under the sofa and bed. I know it's not how my mother would do it, but who cares? When you come right down to it, guys have their mind on one thing, and it's not how clean the house is.

So far I've never gone out with any guy who looks under the furniture. Instead, they usually fantasize about what they'd like to have happen on top of it.

To me, there's always good news and bad news when a boy asks you out. The good part is that ini-

tial reaction of supreme happiness when the guy re-
veals that first spark of interest. The bad news is the
apprehension of whether he really likes you, which
is definitely the case right now. Roger is the sort of
person you can never tell about, and I certainly
conned him into asking me. Another problem is I'm
not sure what I really think of him.

I ought to know about boys. I've gone steady six
times, and obviously it was never everlasting. Four
guys dumped me in a quest for somebody more mature, which is a euphemism for somebody more sex-
ually active. I dumped the others because I never
liked them enough to really be their one and only.

I decide on a jean skirt, white knit top and beads
carved like little animals. It looks arty and not too
impressive. I don't want him to think I'm madly in
love with him and have him start acting like an animal, which boys can do if you give them the wrong
stimuli.

"So where is he taking you?" Mila is getting ready
for a date with Ben. He's taking her to the Chateau
with the fifty-dollar bonus. But she still has her eyes
on Wilber. She's been going down to the Choo-Choo
almost every night.

"A house party."

I like the sound of the words "house party." This
will be the first party in my life where there are no
parents remotely connected with it, which means
Roger won't get the grilleroo when he comes to get

me. I doubt Mila will question him. The idea of it makes me both excited and edgy. I've been to some pretty wild parties, but if you know the person's parents are coming home eventually there are certain things you just don't do.

"A house party?" Mila asks.

"The guys he lives with are having a big party at their place. You can come if you want to. It's an open house."

"Maybe another time. You know, Roger is pretty cute. I like that beard. What are his friends like?"

"I don't know. I'll let you know tomorrow."

Mila watches me put on my makeup. She zips open a blue-and-yellow print Laura Ashley makeup bag. "Why don't you try this Lelane gel blush."

I put down the rouge I got at the drugstore and let Mila make me up. "If you put this copper sparkle on your eyelids, you'll really look sexy." Mila shakes glittery brown shadow onto her fingers and rubs it onto my lids. I thought I knew a lot about emphasizing my best features, but Mila does a better job. By the time she's done I look at least twenty, and Roger is buzzing at the door.

Mila answers it. They chat for a few minutes. When he walks in the door I notice his outfit and can't believe it. He makes me feel overdressed. He's wearing washed-out jeans and an old shirt—the kind of shirt my mother uses for a dust rag—with a jean vest over it. He's also wearing a green visor hat with little buttons that have slogans like Anything Goes, and Let the Good Times Roll written on them.

I look at him for a second. Dressed in tar and feathers he'd still look good. "That's an interesting hat," I tell him.

"This is my pinball hat."

"Your pinball hat?"

"I told you we'd stop at The Greasy Grind. I wanted to shoot a few games. And my games are fabulous whenever I wear this hat."

He surveys me and he surveys Mila. Not that I want Roger to think I'm living with a dripbomb, but I don't like the way he's looking at her. I try not to be jealous. After all, he's hardly her type anyway. She and I have similar features—black hair, blue eyes—and we weigh about the same. But the features are plain old me on me, with or without make-up, and awesome on Mila. She's also wearing a revealing halter-top jumpsuit and lots of provocative perfume. I wonder how far she's gone with Ben. I hate to think about it. I'm sure *he* thinks about it the way she's dressed.

"You're really that into pinball?" I ask Roger as we walk into the hallway that perpetually smells of fish, steak and spaghetti. Sometimes the smell pervades our apartment, so it's impossible to ever forget work.

"You know, Wilber is ordering more machines," Roger answers. "As a matter of fact, he's going to offer one dollar off on games every Monday and Tuesday. Since business is slow those evenings.''

"I see.'' It might also bring in more kids that know me. My stomach does a few flopovers. I have got to find another job fast.

We walk over two blocks south to Pipers Alley, which is a mall containing bars, discos and pinball parlors. I think The Greasy Grind is a combo of all three, which makes me wonder how I'm going to get in. I don't mention it. I'm curious to see what happens.

I'm also trying to figure out a perfect time to talk about Ned and Wilber's, but by the time I feel comfortable we walk into The Greasy Grind, where human voices are barely audible. The girl at the counter checks Roger's ID and doesn't even ask if I have one.

"Hey, how'd you manage that?'' I ask him.

"Don't worry, they pay the cops to leave this place alone. We're not doing anything illegal, like buying booze. We're just going to be here a short time anyhow.''

I hope so. The place is deafening. It's a raucous mixture of bells, sirens and whistles, made more confusing by mirrored walls and flashing lights.

"What's your favorite game?'' Roger asks me.

I'm ready to say "no game.'' I hate pinball. But I see two guys and a girl, named Maggie Wannamaker, from school walking in my direction. I point

to a video game in the opposite corner. I am unable
to avoid them—the girl sat behind me in history.

"Hey, what's happening?" Maggie asks.

"Not much," I answer. I realize it's hard for Roger to hear the conversation, but I'm still feeling nervous.

"You cut the history final. How'd you manage it?" Maggie asks me.

"Oh, I don't know." I'm trying my best to avoid her, but she's one of those talkative types and I can't.

"So what are you doing this summer?"

"Working." I wish she'd disappear. Her voice is getting louder. I realize she has a larynx that adapts to any situation.

"Where?"

"As a waitress. See ya." I grasp Roger and attempt an escape to the corner I originally selected. Maggie walks away and gives me a look of irritation.

Roger points out some games. "Did you mean Commando or Rampage?"

"Rampage." It has prettier pictures on the screen. It's not all red, yellow and black like the rest of the games. It has pictures of a lizard, gorilla and werewolf. A message on the screen says, "destroy the city." It also flashes personality profiles of the animals.

"This is one of my favorites," Roger says. Too bad they don't have it at Wilber's. It's good for relieving frustrations. "Are you good at this?"

"I never tried before."

"Well, which animal do you want to be?"

"How about Lizzie the Lizard?" The two other characters are males. Roger picks George the Gorilla.

The idea is to crumble the buildings on the screen by moving the animals up and down. Roger is skilled at demolishing buildings, he gets 298,000 points. I barely get past 150,000.

"Look," he says, "I'm going to play Commando and Tron. Want to join me?"

I see a few more kids from school playing Evel Knievel near the area that he is pointing towards.

"I think I'll play this for a while." I don't want to take chances on getting into more sticky conversations. There is always the chance that Roger has X-ray hearing or they'll turn the horrible music off. I'm getting kind of attached to my Lizzie the Lizard identity. I also find another game where you pretend to drive a car through some palm trees; I keep running off the road and knocking the trees down.

Finally, Roger decides to get going, which is fine with me. The arcade is boring. I suppose there is some excitement at Greasy's, trying to dodge the people who know me. By that type of thrill is not for me. It gives my stomach that woozy feeling—a feeling I've been getting a lot.

He takes my arm, and we walk out. It's not quite dark yet. It's muggy, and my sandals from Family Footery are not made for long-distance walking, especially after a week at the Choo-Choo.

We walk a few blocks until I ask him, "Where did you park?"

"I don't have a car. I don't like driving. I'm from New York City, and most people there walk or take the subways. Besides, driving pollutes the air. And if people drive too much, oil prices could go up again and put us back into another inflationary recession."

I'm not sure what an inflationary recession is. All I remember is my parents saying something about it a few years ago when I wanted a new ten-speed bicycle. They said the economy was in bad shape and I couldn't have one now. Maybe if I'd listened more closely to the lecture on the crash of 1929 I'd know what to say to Roger.

Finally I decide to bring up the dynamics of Wilber's. It's about all we seem to have in common. "Did you ever notice anything unusual about Wilber's?"

"Like what?" Roger answers as if Wilber's Choo-Choo Express has recently won the Silver Fork Award—the local restaurant industry honor for consistent cleanliness, which my father has won three times.

"You know, the leaky bathroom downstairs, the mess in the basement, and that there's a frayed wire downstairs." I fail to mention the mouse.

"Not really. It's not my business. I do my job for Wilber, and he pays me. That's as far as it goes."

"You mean none of that stuff bothers you?"

"No. Why should it? I don't own the restaurant. I just work there. I've worked in lots of places. They all have their good points and bad points. Wilber is a slob, but he's nice, and he leaves you alone, and his food is good. One guy I worked for was so cheap he had a list of what you could and couldn't eat. Wilber's nice to his employees and lets me play pinball for free when I want. I really feel at home."

"How long have you been working there?"

"Since April, when he opened."

"What about Ned?"

"He started working there around then, too. Come to think of it, he was working there before me. He showed me around."

"He is strange with those sunglasses and hat he always wears. His English is pretty impeccable though, for somebody who dresses like a male bag lady."

"I guess I never thought of it that way. Maybe he wears the glasses to hide his eyes. I bet he's on something. I bet that's it."

"He doesn't seem out of it though. Besides, where would he get money to be on something? He probably doesn't make very much."

"Oh, I don't know. Maybe he sells it on the side. That's it. Maybe he's a drug dealer and the restaurant is a front."

"I really doubt it. That's ludicrous. Of course maybe I'm being ridiculous also. Personally, I think he's smarter than he seems."

"Well, we all have our moments," Roger says. "What makes you think he's so great anyway?"

"I'm intuitive."

"You think so, huh? Now let's see how intuitive you are. We're on my street. Which house do you think is mine?"

The farther we walk, the street gets progressively seedier. It's one of those neighborhoods that you wouldn't dream of going into unless you were doing an architectural study of dilapidated buildings.

I point to an extra ramshackle house, with Lionel Ritchie blaring out of it at three hundred and fifty-five decibels. People in their early twenties, holding beer bottles, are standing on the porch and the overgrown front lawn.

Roger notices me doing a double take.

"I live here because it's economical. I'm paying my own way through college. I have the lease, and other students pay me for the rooms. It's slower in the summer because there're fewer students. But I'm responsible for the place all year."

I imagine this place must be very economical. For me, I'd have to be paid to live there. There's a big crack in the front window, and the paint is peeling. There's a board covering rotted wood on the front steps.

"Hey Roger." A guy who reeks of beer slaps his shoulder. "Where have you been?"

"First I picked up Chris, and then we went to Greasy's to shoot a few rounds. I'm feeling good. I broke my record on Rampage. Chris, this is Eric. One of my housemates."

"Good going." The guy shakes his fist. I'm not sure if "good going" means me or the Rampage game.

Roger shows me inside the house. The living room is strewn with bodies in various states of consciousness. You could get stoned by breathing the air. No matter what state of awareness I would lapse into, it wouldn't matter anyway because Roger could not try one thing on me. There are so many people around we'd have more privacy downtown at rush hour. Roger takes me over to the dining-room table and introduces me to some of the people standing by the table. One couple is glued together.

"This is Dan and this is Beven."

I say "hello." They don't answer. Somehow I don't think if the place blew up that couple would unglue themselves.

"You hungry?" Roger picks up a plate, grabs some pretzels and spoons something over them that looks like cheese that was once melted but is now starting to congeal.

He hands me a plate.

At this point I'm momentarily homesick for parties where the host or hostess's mother takes the time to check whether the refreshments are edible and even helps in the preparation. This food is awful. I wouldn't serve it to a gerbil.

"Want a drink?" he asks.

"Absolutely. I'm dying of thirst." I'm practically salivating. It's a hot night and this place isn't air-conditioned. There's a fan in the room which is doing a better job at blowing the dirty curtains around than cooling us off.

Roger takes me into a kitchen where the linoleum is missing in numerous spots. He opens a refrigerator that was probably the latest model in 1950 and was last defrosted a few years later. "What'll you have?"

"A diet soda."

He looks through the conglomeration of opened food and six-packs of beer cans. "Clean out. Besides, all those chemicals are bad for you."

I can see why he feels so at home at Wilber's. "What else do you have besides beer?"

He hands me an opened bottle of raspberry-apple juice and a pitcher of iced tea with tea bags still floating in it. "It's sun tea," he says.

Under some paper bags on the floor by the refrigerator, I spot a six-pack of Coke Classic.

"I'll have this," I tell him.

"It's warm."

"I'll get myself some ice." I don't usually help myself in people's refrigerators, but in about one second I'm going to die of thirst. The thought of cold Coca-Cola is ambrosial. When I open the freezer to unwedge the ice cube tray, I notice two boxes of Seltro veal cutlets and hot dogs. I don't say a word; my stomach sinks. I take out the ice and pour myself a Coke.

Roger leads me from room to room, where there are groups of people talking to each other, listening to music, or playing board games. Roger selects a room that has the previously glued-together couple now unglued, and other people are playing some unfamiliar game. "This is my room," he tells me.

"Want to play 'Moral Secrets' with us?" a girl with long frizzy hair asks.

The Dan from the unglued couple is the Dan Horvath I knew vaguely from Highland High School.

"I thought Dan was away for the summer," I whisper to Roger.

"Why? Does it matter? He stays at home for the summer to save up money. When school starts he'll be back. Your room upstairs is waiting for you as soon as you're ready," Roger tells Dan.

Dan begins to recognize me. I'm not sure if I should hide in the closet the rest of the evening or leave.

"I don't really want to play 'Moral Secrets,'" I tell Roger.

"C'mon, don't be so uptight. It's fun."

"Yeah, Hadley, stay," Dan says.

"We want to beat your socks off," Eric, the guy who smelled of Eau de Beer Cooler says.

I start to walk out of the room.

"C'mon," Roger chides. "We won't do a thing to embarrass you."

I know when I'm stuck.

"Hey, didn't you go to Highland and Saint Dominic's?" Dan asks.

"Um-hmm." I try not to sound too responsive so maybe he'll leave me alone.

"I bet you know my sister, Tess."

"She's an acquaintance." I'm not about to say she's the girl who was voted most likely to become a nun in third grade and now is the least likely. Tess Horvath has other talents besides making good grades.

"So where are you going now?" he asks.

"I'm not sure yet. I'm working." I'm not about to say I'm a professional waitress. Besides, maybe I'll get a GED and go to junior college. Every day my life seems to be getting more confused, and I feel real uncomfortable at this party. Going to a party with college kids is one thing, but this group is *older* college kids. I don't know if feeling awful at this party or taking a history test would be worse.

Roger and I sit down on the worn carpet. I'm not sure if the purple coloration is a design or stains. We each get dealt five slips of paper with moral questions typed on them and one gray tagboard card. My card says "uncertain" which means I have to ask any person in the group a question to which I think he'll give an ambiguous answer which depends on the circumstances. I don't know a soul well enough, not even Roger, so this isn't going to be easy.

The first person to ask me a question is the girl with the long frizzy hair. "Your neighbor in an adjacent apartment building insists on doing aerobic exercises nude in full view. Do you complain to your neighbor's landlady?"

I laugh. "Are they female or male? If it's a male, is he a hunk?"

"I need a yes or no answer!" she snaps. "We're talking about moral issues."

I can see she is taking the game seriously.

"No, I wouldn't."

Dan asks Beven whether she would not mention she boiled a ham bone in pea soup if one of her guests were a vegetarian, and she'd put a lot of work into the preparation.

Beven says she would tell the truth and offer that person a cheese sandwich.

When it's my turn I ask Roger a question, since he's the only one I know. It's hard to decide which of my questions to ask. Finally I choose one. I can tell everybody is impatient and is playing for blood.

"As an actor, you are asked to do a commercial for a product you can't stand. Do you take the job?" I'm sure he'll say "uncertain." He really seems wishy-washy and not the sort of person who'd commit himself on such a loaded question.

"No, of course not," he answers.

"I challenge you."

"Hey, Hadley's a good guy; he wouldn't take money for something he doesn't believe in," Dan says.

"I don't know," Frizzy Hair answers. "I think he'd do it. I'm sure he'd do it."

"I would not," Roger answers. "I would never endorse anything I didn't like. You're just mad because I challenged you last week when I thought you wouldn't join a terrorist organization for big bucks."

Finally we have a jury. Roger wins; I lose.

Everybody is so stoned or drunk they probably can't think straight. And I want to go back to the apartment. One thing about living with your folks is you can always say you have a curfew when you're in a sticky situation, but now I can't. I'm like a trapped rabbit.

And my mind keeps wandering to what the Swenson guy in the basement office said and where Ned went. Maybe he works in that building. Maybe he lives there. He could be a spy for the government. No, I tell myself. Wilber isn't doing anything that terrible, just a little terrible. But I wonder who reported him to the Board of Health. If he doesn't get the wire fixed soon I'm going to report him myself.

The game is finally over and Dan wins.

Roger and I sit and listen to music for a while. Finally, I'm ready to fall asleep. "Roger, I better get going."

"Hey, can't you just wait till morning? It's a long walk." He kisses me. "You can stay here." He puts his hands in his pockets. "I won't try a thing. You can sleep in the living room."

"No, I have to get home. Find somebody with a car to drive me."

Roger saunters about the house looking for somebody who has a car.

"Hey Dan, before you go back want to give my girl a ride?"

"Sure."

The four of us get into Dan's car. "Good seeing you," he says as he drops me off.

Roger walks me up the stairs. He smells of beer. "I want to do it again soon." He doesn't try to kiss me. Thank God.

What an awful evening. First total boredom and intense noise at Greasy's. Then I find out my date might be pilfering veal cutlets and hot dogs.

I don't ever want to go out with Roger again.

Chapter Eight

In the morning, when I'm returning from the Laundromat, I'm greeted in the hallway by Mila.

"Your father is here," she informs me.

"You must be kidding."

"I wish I were."

I walk into the apartment. He's standing in the living room by the unmade sofa bed, as if I were expecting him and thrilled to see him there.

"It's good to see you," is all that I can muster up. What do you say to a father who has thrown you out of the house due to academic difficulties? This sinking feeling goes through me. The one I get when I know my father is going to give it to me because I've done something that aggravates him.

"See you later." Mila dashes out the door in order to escape the ensuing argument. "There's a special Sunday sale at Pierre Deux today. I'm going to check out the sundresses." She runs down the stairs as if the whole building is going to blow up any second. Which it would in five minutes if words were explosives.

My father scans the apartment. "Is this how I brought you up? To live in this pigsty?"

The only mess is a few dishes in the sink and the magazines sticking out from under the sofa. Somehow I don't think he's in the mood to argue about degrees of messiness, so I don't try to explain.

He's shouting so loud that the tenant next door to us taps on the wall. I swear my father has the most well-developed lungs in North America.

"How could you quit school and be a waitress at that dump downstairs? What do you want to be? A nobody? You're coming home now." He grabs clothes from the closet and throws them into a suitcase. Some of them are Mila's.

"What are you doing?" I grab a Gucci scarf and pair of Sassoon slacks from him.

"I'm packing up your things. The car's waiting."

"I'm not leaving." I hate to be pressured, and his tactics are ensuring I'll never return.

"You can work for me the rest of the summer if you like waiting on tables so much. I'll teach you everything I know. Then you'll go back to school in the fall and finish up. I can't even face the neighbors and tell them what you did with yourself."

"Look, I'll never make it in school. I don't want to go back." The whole thought of facing Mr. Luella makes me ill. By now it's probably all over the high-school community that Chris Pattinos quit school, which is a very unusual thing to do at Highland High School. I'd absolutely crumble from embarrassment if all the kids questioned me about why I came back.

My father waves his hands in the air. For a minute I think that he's going to hit me. I dodge him and fall on the sofa.

"The reason you no do well is you no try. That's why you no make it. You try and you make it in America. I have two stores and a house paid for and I don't do it by sitting on my backside. I did it because I take classes as soon as I get here. It was hard work."

I can tell my father is really upset because he hardly ever talks with bad grammar unless he's really blown away. The last time he sounded like that was when his father died in Ohio, and at the funeral home they demanded cash instead of a check.

"I've hardly been sitting around watching soap operas all day." I'm ready to take off my shoes and show him all my blisters, which have increased considerably since last night's walk.

He pulls at my arm. "You come with me now!"

"No!" I'm defiant. "I'm not going. You can't make me."

He lets go of my arm. "You know if I want I can have the truant officer out after you in the fall. I could even report you as a runaway and have the police come any minute. They'd put you into a juvenile detention home."

"I'd like to see you try it anyway." I know it's something he'd never do.

He could never live with himself if he knew he was responsible for sending me to some place where I'd have to sleep in a dormitory with teen murderers, prostitutes and thieves. And I'd hardly think they'd do something like that for someone who barely qualifies as a runaway. I wonder if they still serve bread and water at those places. I've read a lot about that in books.

He bangs his fist on the rickety table. It breaks. His face turns red. I don't know whether I should laugh or cry.

"Okay, don't come home. Do it your way. I disown you now! Your name is out of my will. I never want to see you again. I don't consider you my daughter." My father bursts out of the door, slams it and stomps down the stairs.

I feel horrible, but not horrible enough to go home.

My father has a terrible temper and doesn't always mean what he says. One time he threatened to rip out the phone because Kathi and I were on it so much. Another time, after he found out I forged his name on my report card, his threat of eternal grounding lasted less than a month.

I'm too confused, and need space right now. I have mixed feelings about absolutely everything in my life. Everything would be so tense at my folks' that a case of debilitating beriberi wouldn't encourage my return home. I go to the window and watch my father drive away.

A few minutes after he leaves, my mother calls. "Could you remind Daddy to pick up a carton of milk and some juice before you two come home?"

"He left already."

"He what?" She sounds as if I've told her he's run off with another woman.

"Just what I said, he left already. I'm not coming home."

"How could you do that?" She starts screaming something unintelligible.

When she's finally done, I tell her, "I'll come home if and when I'm ready."

She emits a sigh of maximum annoyance and slams the receiver down. As soon as I'm done with her, there's a knock on the door. I'm sure it's my father to continue the argument. It's not.

It's an old man wearing an outfit that looks as if it were color coordinated by a parrot. He's wearing green plaid pants and a bright yellow polyester shirt that fits snugly around his belly. The bottom button doesn't close well, and I can see an unappetizing view of skin.

"Who are you?" he asks me as if I'm an alien from another planet.

"Chris Pattinos. I'm Mila's cousin and roommate."

"Well, I don't know what was going on in here and I don't care here. It ain't my affair. But keep your personal business to a mild roar, and I need to know your name and place of employment."

"What for?"

"For my records. I'm the building manager. My name is Augie. Augie Martin."

He walks into the living room while I write down the information and hand it to him on a sheet of perfumed paper that says "Lelane . . . we're only as good as you are."

He reads it over. "So you're working for Wilber. He's a good tenant. Doesn't cause no trouble. Of course, he hasn't been there that long. Hope for your sake he stays around. Restaurants come and go, you know. That cousin of yours, she don't cause no trouble either, except always being late with her rent.

Maybe with you here, she'll pay the rent on time for once."

"You mean she's never paid on time?" By now I'm not really surprised.

"Not yet. But she's only been here a few months. She wears fancy shmancy clothes and with that car of hers I think she's living above her means. Anyhow, it ain't my business, as long as she pays. But I wish I didn't always have to bother her about it. It's a lot of trouble and then I have to assess late charges. Nice meeting you."

"Same here."

I look out the window, watch the trucks and buses go by, and cry. After I'm all drained, Mila walks in the door with a bag from Pierre Deux.

"So how'd it go with your dad?" she asks. She opens the phone book, pulls out her bills and looks at them apprehensively.

"It was a slice. He threatened to disown me. What happened with you and your folks when you decided to leave?" I'm too upset to start asking her about the rent. I have enough problems of my own.

Mila makes out a check and sticks it into an envelope. "My folks were kind of glad in a way. We had five kids in a small house, and my dad had just been sacked from his job. As soon as I graduated and started working full-time, my mom wanted me to pay her rent. She thought if I had money for nice clothes, I should pay her room and board. Besides, I was sick of sharing a room with my two sisters. I wanted peace and quiet for a change. And if I feel like buying myself nice things instead of schlock, it's up to me. Not my mom.''

I think of my own room at home. It's small but I do have my own bathroom that I share with Kathi. Her room is on the other side of my wall.

"Anyway it's hard sometimes being on my own." Mila looks sad for a second. "I think I better level with you. I don't work full-time for Lelane Cosmetics. I work for United Pharmaceuticals as a secretary and sell Lelane products on the side. When I first started working I was at Lelane but they didn't pay so well. So Mrs. O. got me this job at United. I decided to make extra money by selling Lelane."

"How come you didn't tell me?"

"I don't know." She shrugs her shoulders. "Anyway I'm telling you now because you'd find out soon enough. It's a good second income. If you ever want to try it, let me know."

Knowing Mila, she'll get an extra payment if I decide to do it, which really ticks me off.

I'm not all that shocked by Mila's revelation and smug in feeling I'm probably making almost as much as her with one job.

"By the way," Mila says, "my white suit. I'll need it this week. I have two new customers that want to see some Lelane products and I need to look ritzy for them. Appearance is very important. Especially in sales.''

"I'll pick it up tomorrow," I tell her.

She stacks up her pile of paid bills. ''Please don't forget. You're sure they said it will come back okay?''

"That's what they told me when I brought it in. Don't worry about it.''

I spend the rest of Sunday feeling guilty and wondering when my father will speak to me again. I remember the times he's been extra nice to me, like the time I lost my stuffed rabbit at a movie theater and he went back and got it for me. The time my canary died he wrote me an absence note saying there was a death in the family. He got me a parakeet the next day. I think of all the times me and Kathi baked birthday cakes for him—one of the few times we didn't fight with each other.

Then I go over to the park. I sit and watch the bag ladies and the families on picnics. I walk over to the south end by the lake and look at the fancy buildings. I wonder which one Ned went into. He probably works in one. Maybe he isn't really as bright as he seems. What a life!

By morning I'm almost too upset to go to work. It's probably a side effect of feeling guilty. But I go, of course. Unfortunately, there's one difference between cutting work and school. If you cut school you just have to make up the work. If you cut work you don't get paid and can lose your job. And I need the money. I hope there's not a rash of takeouts this morning. It's a pain to pack them, and take-out customers don't always leave a tip.

I'm greeted by Ned who is washing the floor as usual. Where we walk is one part of Wilber's that isn't a health hazard. Sometimes Ned seems like a floor-washing robot and other times he seems so smart.

I get to work on cutting lemons and counting the money in the register. A few minutes before we open Lou knocks on the door. He's the last person I want to see. Actually, I don't want to see anybody, especially customers. I'm not in the mood to toddle around smiling with toast, coffee and eggs.

"So what are you doing here so bright and early?"

"Just thought I'd stop by and tell you I'd consider your big idea for a later issue. *Capisci* and *comprèndi*?"

I wink at him.

"But for now I'm going to do an article on street fairs." He hands me some typewritten sheets. I read it over. "If I were mayor we'd get a fair share of fun and profit with annual street fairs." Lou looks around the restaurant for a minute. "Now I'll have a Crazy Omelette."

"Did anybody ever tell you your stomach was made of iron?"

"Rustproof," he answers.

The phone rings. Ned answers it. He takes the phone into the back. After he hangs up he comes over to me. "I hate to break up the party, but the boss man is on his way."

"He doesn't usually come in until later." I place Lou's order on the spindle.

"The health inspector is coming today to check this place out," Ned informs me.

"It could sure use it."

"You think so?" He looks at me as if we have had a simultaneous divine revelation.

"This place is out of whack," I tell him. "First of all, those games don't have a city license. The basement looks like a firetrap and that cooler downstairs is filthy. To name a few things." I don't mention anything about Swing-it Swenson because it's something I overheard and if by any chance there is a Swedish Mafia I don't want to be on their hit list. I'm also sorry I mentioned the cooler because I don't want to be elected to clean it out.

"I know just what you mean." Ned takes a rag and polishes the soda fountain. "Not everybody notices that stuff, though. You're an observant girl." He smiles at me and starts to go downstairs. "Look, why don't you man, I mean woman, the counter and tables upstairs. And I'll get the place together as fast as I can. It shouldn't be too busy this morning. The restaurant in the Crossroads Hotel is reopening. And those paver people are gone."

I feel about a third of my day's tips evaporate rapidly away. Except for a few straggling customers the place is pretty slow. I glance at Lou reading his *Youth in Government Handbook*. "It's time to go." Lou hops off the stool. He takes his helmet and carefully puts it on his head. "I'm taking Anne Marie for the best air-conditioned ride in town after work today."

"I'm sure she has a monogrammed helmet especially for the big occasion." I put Lou's plates in the bus pan and wipe off the counter.

"I'll order her one for her debutante party," he answers. "Compliments of L.P."

Lou rushes out the door, and I can hear the roar of his Harley. I wish I could run out the door, jump on the back and ride away somewhere. Somewhere where I'd have no problems ever again.

Ned tosses me a rag. "So the place at least looks nice."

"Looks can be deceiving."

It's so slow without the convention and boring without Roger. I keep hoping things will pick up.

When Wilber comes in he doesn't look too worried. Maybe he's not the type to worry about anything. I wish I were like that. But I've been a worrier since birth. He goes straight into the back where the bar is and closes the door. I hear a clanking of glasses and water running. It seems as though he's at least trying to make the place presentable. Maybe I was imagining him trying to pay the inspector off.

A little later, three customers come in. Two sit at the counter and one sits at a booth alone. The one sitting alone opens his wallet and shows me his badge. "I'm Phil Wagner from the Department of Health. Mr. Larsen is expecting me."

I knock on the door to the bar. "Wilber, your guest is here to see you."

Wilber saunters out as if Mr. Wagner were a Hollywood talent scout and Wilber were auditioning for a movie. "You're just the person I've been waiting for."

"You haven't had a full inspection yet, so we'll need to see everything."

"Want to see the lounge first or the basement?"

They go back into the bar. Wilber closes the door between the bar and restaurant section of the Choo-Choo so I can't hear what's going on. I'm stuck anyway since Ned has disappeared as usual. That basement is a mess, so he probably needs a while to clean it. Roger is right; Ned is weird. But I like him. He's probably just a person who's down on his luck.

Next Mr. Wagner and Wilber go down to the basement.

Ned comes up a little later.

"Ned, is it okay if I ask you a question?"

"Sure, as long as it's not about my height or weight," he answers.

"Did you ever work at any other places?"

"Yes, I did a while back," he answers thoughtfully.

"What places did you work at?"

"Imperial Lanes and the Do Drop Inn to name a few. Why are you so interested in me anyhow?" He seems surprised and a bit irritated.

"I don't know; I was curious. Like I said before, this place is bizarre."

"Why are you so interested in how Wilber runs his business? You planning on buying a place of your own?"

"I guess I don't want to contribute to a plague of botulism."

"Don't worry. There won't be any botulism. I promise."

A few minutes later Wilber and Mr. Wagner look over the fountain area. Mr. Wagner lifts up the containers of maple syrup and holds them up to the light. "You know there are foreign particles in here, too?"

"Not again," Wilber whispers. He looks gloomy.

"Just like in the liquor. Fruit flies are very attracted to sugary substances."

I'm so disgusted I'm ready to barf. The two of them go into the kitchen, which isn't too bad except for pieces of cabbage and lettuce that have fallen on the floor. I follow them and pretend to be in the upstairs bathroom. This is too interesting to miss.

"Well, some other guys might turn you in, but I'll let it pass," Mr. Wagner says. "You can salvage everything by pouring it through the coffee filters."

The two go back downstairs.

I stand on the landing in order to hear them.

"Thanks," Mr. Wagner says. I don't have to be intuitive to know that Wilber just gave Wagner an envelope. "You know there was this other place a few blocks from here. As soon as the guy saw my badge he told me where to go. So I wrote up more violations for him than bar stools. But you're a nice guy. You made it easy for me and I'll make it easy for you. Be glad this isn't an electrical inspection—that wire might give you problems."

I'd love to report him. But who would I report him to? The health department might send him out again. But I'm going to report that wire. Maybe that will fix Wilber's fixes.

"Hey!" Ned comes up from nowhere. "Don't you have some people to wait on?"

Ruth is right. Ned absolutely comes out of the woodwork.

"Sure."

I go back to work and can't stop thinking about that wire, and I've got fruit flies on the brain. The place has gotten busier now so I'm really running here and there.

As soon as I get off work I pick up Mila's suit. All the spots are out. It looks perfect. At least something is going right. I pick up a newspaper. I've got to find something else! But there are only two waitress jobs in the classifieds. One has already been filled and the other needs somebody who can serve liquor and wear a brief uniform. I seriously consider researching welfare.

As soon as I get home, I call the fire department about the wire.

"Oh," says the lady on the other end. "That's the second complaint we've had recently. We were sure that would have been taken care of by now. We had an inspector out and he okayed it. We'll send somebody out again."

I get to the Choo-Choo at six-thirty the next morning and go straight into the bar. Then I stick my finger in some ouzo just to taste it. Gross. Who would want to drink any of this—with or without fruit flies in it? Then I pour cognac, Drambuie, blended whiskey and every other bottle of sweet liquor down the drain. I replace the ones I can with bottles from underneath the liquor cabinet and hide the empty bottles in the dumpster. I also get rid of the maple syrup.

Ben will really earn his fifty dollars for an "extra" pickup this time around.

Chapter Nine

Mila is not satisfied with the suit when she goes to put it on the next morning.

"There's still a spot above the pocket," she gripes.

I take the suit under the light and examine it carefully. I pretend that I'm a health inspector checking for fruit flies.

The only spot I see is the faint beige spot the size of a dime. It looks like it's part of the weave of the suit, and can be easily covered by a handkerchief. And Mila always properly folds and presses her hankies before she puts them into her suit pockets.

"I don't know if I can wear it like this," she

whines, as if it were covered with spots and ripped. "You should have been more careful."

"C'mon, Mila," I tell her, "the suit is fine." It would be fine for me, anyway.

"I'm glad you think so."

"You have so many outfits, can't you wear something else?"

"I wanted to wear that suit today. I'm seeing three people after work who want to buy Lelane. And I need to look perfect."

"Mr. Miracle Clean is one of the best dry cleaners around," I tell her. They said that was the best they could do, and it looks pretty good to me.

She looks at the suit again despondently. "Maybe if I take it over there on the way to work they'll clean it again."

"That's a good idea, but they'll probably tell you that there isn't anything wrong with it." I can't believe that she's acting so off-the-wall. I'm not telling her just to get out of reimbursing her, but the suit looks like something I'd be thrilled to own, even though I'd have no place to wear it.

Mila puts on a navy-blue suit that is identical to the white one. I'm glad I basically like the simple things in life. Sometimes I think fancy clothes are important, but frankly I'd rather have stuff that's no big deal if it gets stained or ripped. I'd get ulcers if I had to deal with such an expensive wardrobe or Mila's pile of bills. I walk out of the door to go to the Choo-Choo. "Bye, Mila, have a nice day."

She doesn't say a word.

When I get to work I'm greeted by Roger. "What are you doing here? I thought you weren't working mornings anymore."

"Wilber called and said he needed me this morning. He's madder than a hornet. He mentioned something about somebody swiping his liquor. I hope he doesn't consider me a suspect, since I had a party recently."

My heart is beating like an alarm clock. "Where's Ned?"

"I don't know. Maybe he got canned. Maybe Wilber thinks he stole the liquor. Wilber sounded real strange this morning. And you and I," Roger says, "need to have a little talk about something."

"Believe me I won't snitch about the veal cutlets or hot dogs."

"What veal cutlets and hot dogs?"

"The ones I saw in your freezer."

"Don't you think it would be pretty difficult to walk out of here with two twenty-five pound boxes of frozen meat? For your information, I bought the stuff from Wilber when the supplier came in here. Why don't you mind your own business? I bet you think you're pretty smart for a high school kid, don't you?"

I'm shocked but pretend not to hear him. I take a metal tray of Jell-O out of the case and spoon the squares into serving dishes.

"Don't play games. Dan Horvath remembered you. He even checked it out in his sister's yearbook. You're not supposed to graduate until next June. How old are you anyway? I want to know this minute."

"I'm sixteen. I'll be seventeen in October."

"Why didn't you tell me the truth when I interviewed you?"

"Because I needed the money, that's why. I needed to find a job so I could support myself fast."

"Did you run away from home? I never dated a runaway before and I'm not starting now."

"I didn't run away from home." I take three pies out of the case and put them down on the counter to cut into wedges. "My folks know exactly where I am."

"You mean you aren't leaving after the summer is over?"

"I didn't say I was leaving or not leaving. And yes, I did quit school."

"So you can live a life like Ned?"

"Maybe I won't live a life like Ned. My life is my problem. What do you care so much about it for anyway?"

"For one thing, your little show could have gotten me into big trouble. What if we'd have gotten caught in The Greasy Grind? Eighteen is one thing, but sixteen and one-half is another. I could have gotten in trouble for contributing to the delinquency of a minor."

"Well, we didn't get caught in The Greasy Grind. As you remember, we waited until we got to your house until we had anything to drink. As you explained, the cops are paid off to leave Greasy's alone anyway. So what difference does it make?"

"It made plenty of difference. You weren't being honest with me. I have the lease on my house. What if it got raided and everybody picked up?"

"Then maybe you should have parties that can't possibly get raided." I'm so upset that I couldn't care less about Roger and his paranoia. "Could you answer one question for me. Why do you think Ned isn't here this morning?"

"The only logical explanation is that Wilber thinks he ripped off the liquor."

I wish I could escape now, find Ned and talk to him. The poor guy is without a job, and it's probably all my fault.

A customer walks in. "Could you two have your lovers' quarrel out of the restaurant? I'm hungry."

I'm ready to quit but I can't. I really need the money, especially with Mila on the warpath about that suit. Today and yesterday have really been slow.

Wilber comes in a little later, goes over to the cash register, takes some receipts out and goes down to his office. I'm tempted to tell him about the liquor, but don't have the nerve. Maybe I can find Ned, bring him back here and then tell Wilber. I'm so confused I don't know what to do. The entire day I keep mixing up orders and drop a hot roast beef sandwich on the floor.

"What's buggin' you?" Roger asks. "Are you the one who ripped off the liquor?"

"Of course not!" My heart does its alarm-clock beating exercise for the second time today. It's not as if I'm exactly lying. I poured it out because it was gross and I didn't want anyone to get sick.

"Do you know anything about Ned, like where he lives?" I ask Roger before he leaves. "You two started working here about the same time."

"How would I know? I told you he's weird. He probably lives at some fleabag hotel. Why don't you mind your own business?"

I ask Ruth and the other waitresses about Ned, but nobody knows. I've got to find him, tell him how sorry I am and that it's all my fault. It's amazing—I try to do something right and it goes wrong. Roger is right. I should mind my own business. But until this is settled, I'm going to have to mind both my business and a little bit of Ned's. I remember he mentioned working at the Do Drop Inn and Imperial Lanes. Maybe somebody there knows something about him.

I go over to the Do Drop Inn and ask for the manager. I try to ignore the drunks leering at me in my short uniform. After one glance they all sip their drinks and go back to what they are watching on the big-screen TV.

"Did a little guy named Ned work here?"

"He did, but he quit a while ago. He said he had some priorities to take care of. You a friend of his?" the man asks.

"I know him from work."

The man puts his hand on his head and thinks for a minute. "He said it was something urgent he needed to tend to. I'm surprised he didn't give some sort of notice."

"Why?"

"Well, he was a good worker. I was thinking he might like to fill in as bartender sometime. Hope he gets his problems solved."

"You don't happen to have his address or phone number do you?"

"No, I don't believe so. But if you do run into him, tell him that George at the Do Drop says the job is always open."

I go over to Ambassador Lanes. A lady with white hair and a polka-dot dress is standing by the entrance.

"Is there a guy named Ned who used to work here? I was wondering if you knew where he lived."

"No, I never got any specs on him." The lady pulls me aside. "You know we always paid him cash. That's how he wanted it. He was a very lovely man, always punctual and polite."

"Do you by any chance have his phone number?"

"He didn't have a phone."

Then I think of one last possibility.

I walk over to city hall and look for Lou. A man in the hallway directs me to the Youth Project office. I'm greeted by Anne Marie who is sitting at a desk and looking over some papers. "Hello there," she says. "Are you okay? You look as if you've lost your last friend."

"I lost one of them. Where's Luigi?"

"He's in the back room stamping tax bills."

The minute he sees me he pulls up a chair for me. "What's wrong?"

"Remember when I asked you to follow Ned?"

"Yeah."

"Well, he disappeared. I think Wilber fired him or threatened to fire him because he thinks Ned ripped off some liquor, but I'm the one who ripped it off."

Lou puts down the papers he's been stamping and puts his hands on his eyebrows. "Are you bonkers? First you quit school, then you leave home. Now you're stealing. I didn't even know you drank! Do you have a subconscious desire to go to juvenile hall or something?"

"I didn't drink it. I dumped it out because it had fruit flies in it, and Wilber was going to keep it and strain the flies through the coffee filters."

"Run that by me again." Lou looks at me as if I've told him the story in Swahili.

I repeat the story. "What time do you get out of here? I have to know the exact building you saw Ned go into. I've got to find him. I may have cost him his job at Wilber's."

"I'm not sure. Maybe it was that tall one with the glassy front. I'd have to see it again." He walks over to a watercooler. "You look as if you could use something cold." He hands me some Randall and Putney distilled water. "Why don't you just wait? I'll help you find that Ned guy as soon as I'm off."

As soon as work is over Lou and I hop on his cycle, and he drives me over to the south side of Mundelein Park.

"Maybe it was that building," he says. "The Edgewater. It was hard to tell because a truck drove by and obscured my vision."

"Maybe I should go over to the building and ask the doorman if Ned lives or works here."

Lou looks at me. "Maybe I should go ask. I'm wearing a shirt and tie, and to tell you the truth I'm not sure which building it is."

"I look like such a mess they'd probably never tell me anything anyway," I answer. I can feel my eye makeup running, and my hair feels like damp string.

Lou goes across the street. I sit on the curb and close my eyes. It takes him a while. By the clock on the savings and loan, it takes almost a half hour. Finally Lou comes back. He's carrying two sno-cones that he bought from one of the park vendors.

"So what did you find out?"

"*Nada*. Do you want the cherry or Tahiti punch cone?"

I take the Tahiti punch one from him. "You mean they wouldn't give you any information?"

"No, they were very nice. I went to all six buildings. They've never seen such a man."

"Are you serious?" I'm ready to break out in tears.

"Look, Chris, somebody like Ned is probably used to crazy bosses and losing jobs. Maybe he just stopped in a building to use the drinking fountain. Or maybe I was wrong. Why don't I take you home now?"

He hands me a helmet, and I hop on the back of his cycle.

"Look," he says as he drops me off, "don't worry, and remember what I said about Ned. You did what you thought was right."

"Well, it sure backfired."

I go upstairs, peel off my clothes and take a shower. As soon as I'm done I go down to the Choo-Choo.

Wilber is by the register, and Roger is playing Pin Bot during the predinner lull.

"Wilber, I need to talk to you right now."

"What's the problem?"

"I'm responsible for the liquor. I dumped it down the drain."

"Why did you do that?" Wilber asks incredulously. "It was perfectly good booze."

"Because it was full of fruit flies. You can't go around cutting corners all the time and paying people off."

Wilber looks at me as if I've just handed him a three-eyed contact-lens case. Roger looks at me as though I'm off-the-wall.

"I quit!" I walk out of the restaurant and up the stairs, convinced I've done the right thing. I don't want to work for a person like Wilber. So what if the money is good. I start getting my things together and pack them in my suitcase.

When Mila gets home, she's holding the suit right in front of me.

"The cleaner said they did all they could with the suit."

"That's the same thing they said to me. The suit is fine. I've got more on my mind than a suit right now. Could we shelve it?"

"It's a matter of opinion about the suit." Mila throws the suit on the sofa as if it were a rag.

"Whose opinion?"

"Your opinion because it is now your suit."

"Mine?"

"And I expect you to reimburse me the way you said you would."

"I said I'd reimburse you only if I ruined the suit, and I didn't ruin it."

"I wouldn't be caught dead in it right now. And I think you're pretty childish not to pay your debts."

I continue packing my things and stuff the suit into my suitcase.

"Where are you going anyway?" Mila asks.

"Home! You can live in a place that smells like a school cafeteria if you want."

I call a cab. All this hassle is much worse than school. I've had it. Mila doesn't try to stop me or take the suit from me. She probably thinks I'm going to pay her for it and she's sadly mistaken.

My mother is home, sitting in the kitchen doing a crossword puzzle. She breaks out in tears. "This is a very happy day! I can't wait to call your father!" I break out in tears, too, but it's not from happiness; they're from frustration.

About ten minutes later, my father arrives home from work.

He doesn't say much except, "Tomorrow at four o'clock you can start working for me, and I expect you to plan on finishing school."

I realize I need to go back and finish, yet there is this bizarre part of my psyche that feels horrendous and embarrassed about giving up my master plan.

Chapter Ten

That was three weeks ago. It's amazing how what I thought was going to be the most sensational summer of my life has turned out to be the most abysmal one of my existence. It would probably break the Richter scale abominability index. It's that bad.

The worst part is that I have to spend the rest of the summer filling in at my father's restaurant for waitresses who are on vacation. My hours are four in the afternoon until eleven in the evening, Wednesday through Sunday. My father should be reported for cruel and unusual punishment to a minor. The setup is what I call sneakily grounding me, although I get paid like everyone else. My father and I presently have an employer-employee relationship; he treats me like any other waitress, except a little less cordially. Otherwise he treats me like I have contagious cholera or malaria.

The only time he converses with me is to notify me when there's somebody at my station or to take care of the register. He has told me I'm a good waitress, but that's about it. Basically I'm like a combination boarder and prisoner in my own house. The only reason my mother talks to me is because Kathi is gone and she doesn't have any other female to talk to, unless she wants to converse with our bird.

Kathi just wrote me a letter yesterday.

Dear Chrissy:

I'm so glad you're going to be home when I get there. I promise I'll do the best to get along with you. I bought you a present. You'll love it. School isn't so bad. It's no worse than working here. I have to do everything. Be happy you stayed home and didn't get stuck going to Devil's Lake. Mrs. Kaufman is a slave driver. I don't have time to flirt with anybody. This job is the pits.

Love,
Kathi

I suppose when your whole world has collapsed

around you, even a letter from a bratty sister sounds good.

She doesn't know what the pits are until she works for our father. Needless to say his operation isn't as lackadaisical as Wilber's Choo-Choo, which was closed for remodeling not long after that horrible day I decided to throw in the towel. I still say the place and Ned were bizarre. Something did not jibe about the place or Ned. I wish I'd have stayed on a little longer to find out.

You could eat off the floor at my dad's place. Everybody is in charge of cleaning up—blood relatives included. I've become very adept at mopping the floor.

One day while I'm singing "Happy Birthday" to a group that has ordered an extra-large Belly Buster pizza with thirteen candles on it, a man who looks like the Ned double I saw in the Aphosdel Bookstore walks in. This Ned double is not wearing khakis and a polo shirt. He's wearing the kind of striped navy suit your father wears if he's a lawyer or an accountant, or sells something that's expensive.

The man walks up to my father and opens his wallet to show him something. As soon as my father sees the something, they chat for a few minutes, and the Ned double sits at a table by the kitchen, near the back. Then, as if the man were the king of England, my father rushes into the kitchen and returns with a submarine sandwich and a pitcher of root beer. Both of them eye me curiously, as if I'd just split my skirt.

Of course, I'm dying to go back there and see what's going on. But the second my feet turn in that direction, five guys in dirty baseball suits walk in and act as if they haven't had anything to eat or drink since last August.

My father comes up to me while I'm pouring the guys' Coke into the pitcher. "William Nedlon Carther from the *Northside Journal* wants to see you. He's sitting at the back table. He says you two know each other."

William Nedlon Carther is the reporter who started with the *Journal* when he was sixteen. He's lived in homeless shelters to study the poor, and practically got killed when he posed as a dealer while doing an exposé on dope. I'm so blown away that I practically spill the Coke. I'm not so dumb after all. Of course, in any conversations with him, I will leave out the part about following him.

As I near the back table I still can't believe that this guy is or was Ned. He was the guy in the bookstore!

"What do you need me for?" I sit down, and he pours us both a glass of root beer.

Before he can tell me anything, a family of seven complete with sound-barrier-breaking infants and cranky toddlers walks in.

Mr. Carther takes a sip of root beer. "Do you think we could leave for a few minutes?" He seems ill at ease.

I tell my father I'm going out for a while. He doesn't make a fuss.

Mr. Carther leads me to a beige Honda hatchback in the parking lot and turns on the air-conditioning in the car.

I'm so excited I can't stand it. "You were investigating Wilber's Choo-Choo, weren't you? Why did *he* get selected? I bet corruption was the reason you conducted a probe."

"You're right about the reason for the investigation. New restaurants have more inspections and are most vulnerable to payoffs. That's one of the reasons why Wilber's was the subject." He's silent for a moment. "I'm wondering if I could interview you for the special 'Eat and Run' series we're going to run. You could discuss how easily the payoff system works. I already talked to your dad. He's given me permission to use your name."

"You want *me* to give an interview?"

"I'd like that very much. You're a bright young lady. I bet you want to be an investigative reporter yourself."

"I don't know what I'm going to do, yet," I tell him.

He looks surprised. "Anyway, about that interview, could you come in to the *Journal* office tomorrow?"

"Exactly what is the series going to be about?"

"I have a copy of what's going in as the kick-off article. I'll show it to you." He reaches in the back for his briefcase, opens it and hands me some papers.

Special Series
Eat and Run

In city and suburban restaurants, there are sometimes more violations than cockroaches. In a recent investigation by a *Northside Journal* staff member, flagrant infractions of regulations were found due to a system that allows payoffs, tax fraud, gross uncleanliness and illegal kickbacks, which will be exposed in our Eat and Run series.

Today the *Northside Journal* brings you the first in its month-long series by award-winning undercover investigative staff member, William Nedlon Carther.

I don't even go into reading the text of the article I'm so angry, but I do notice the words *award winning*.

"This article makes the entire restaurant industry look like it's a total scam. That's not true. My dad's place is a clean operation. He won the Silver Fork Award and third prize in the Midwest Thin-Crust Pizza Championship. You can only interview me under one condition.''

"What condition? Knowing you, it's probably an interesting one." I can tell he's trying hard to stifle a smile or a laugh.

"I want to write an article expressing another view of the situation. I remember from civics class that's my intrinsic right."

"You're right and you're wrong." Mr. Carther throws his briefcase into the back seat. "You do have a right to express your view, but a newspaper is only obligated to publish it in 'Letters to the Editor'—and I'm sure we'll be getting plenty of public opinion over this series. I'll tell you what. You write it. If it's up to quality, I'll see about printing it. Bring it in tomorrow."

"Seriously?" Not that I thought he'd say no, but he seems pretty agreeable.

"Sure, if it's good enough I'll see that it gets printed. Make sure it's short because it will only be a sidebar. After all, printing both sides of a story is good and fair journalism. You'll learn all about that if that's what you decide to major in at college. Make it early because I've got a story I'm going on later. I'm sure hoping I'll get that interview from you."

"So do I," I answer. But he only gets it if my sidebar article is printed. I refuse to budge on that point. I'm not going to do anything to make the industry my father has worked so hard in look bad. I start to get out of the car.

Ned rolls down the window. "By the way, I'm curious about why a girl whose father owns such a nice establishment would be working at Wilber's and live above it. Wouldn't it have been more economical to live at home and work at your daddy's place for the summer?"

My instincts tell me William Nedlon Carther worked on newspapers part-time before he graduated high school. I'll bet Mila's entire wardrobe he never considered quitting school at sixteen, and I certainly would never divulge to him my previous intentions. "That's personal. You're an investigative reporter. I bet you could figure that out."

As soon as I return to the restaurant my father comes over to me. "So what kind of story was Mr. Carther from the *Journal* here to see you about?"

"Could you trust me for once? I can't tell you yet." I look him straight in the eyeballs. I hear you can charm snakes that way. I wonder if it applies to fathers. "You'll find out soon enough."

"That's not a very good answer." He eyeballs me back.

"Well at this time it's the best answer I have for you. Let's put it this way. I'm two hundred percent glad I'm going back to school in the fall. I'll have no regrets."

"That's the most sensible thing you've said in a long time." He goes into the kitchen and starts spinning pizza dough, and I go back to work thinking of what I'm going to write. My mind is intense on the article, but I don't spill, drop or mix up any orders.

As soon as I get home from work I go into the attic to search for our old Smith Corona portable. My folks used to use it to type up stuff for the business, but now they use a computer instead. My banging around wakes up my mother, who comes running up the stairs wearing her nightgown, flip-flops and a little blue nylon cap. She's one of those women who gets her hair done every week and is petrified to crush it.

"What are you doing? It's after midnight. You're waking up the whole house."

"I'm looking for something!"

"Look for it quietly or wait until tomorrow. Maybe you can prance around till sunup. But your poor father and I need our sleep."

"It's important and I'm not prancing."

I find the typewriter under some old baby clothes, Christmas tree ornaments and outgrown Halloween costumes. I hit the keys sharply to see if the typewriter is still among the living. It works. Except the *k*, the *w* and the *l* stick and leave black marks, unless I tap them carefully.

After about fifteen different drafts and over a hundred typing errors, I finally come up with my sidebar.

Sometimes Money Can Buy Everything.
Or Can It?

The *Journal* "Eat and Run" series has certainly done a commendable job of illustrating how easy it is to "buy" cleanliness, safety and dishonest bookkeeping procedures. While the Choo-Choo Express and other small businesses have shown themselves to succumb to payoffs instead of correcting violations, this is not true of all small businesses.

Having been involved in the restaurant business for a number of years, I know that my father's business, Perry Pattinos Pizza Parlour, makes good profits without cutting corners. I'm sure he's not the only such operation.

It is unfortunate that some owners do fall victim to a system that is corrupt and makes other owners look bad.

I set my alarm and wake up bright and early to meet Mr. Carther. Hopefully he'll take it. If the *Journal* wants to ream the restaurant business, that's their problem, but I'm going to have a chance to say what I think.

I decide to look professional. I press Mila's white suit and put it on with a blue-print, floppy-bow blouse I hardly ever wear. I search through my jewelry box for a pair of earrings. I consider wearing the rhinestone drop earrings but choose some tiny gold loops instead. I suppose I did learn something from Mila.

Then I run out the door to the bus stop. I see a woman get on who is wearing an apron that says Eddie's Barbecue and white shoes. I feel sorry for her. Not that there is anything wrong with being a waitress. But it's hot, messy work, and I'd rather do something else with my life. I might as well give myself a fair chance. I think about Ned's persona as Mr. Carther and Ned as William Nedlon Carther. I suppose Mila is right about appearance being important, but I know now it takes more than that.

The bus stops right in front of the *Northside Journal* which is down the street from the *Suburban Press*. The two papers are competitors; the only difference is the *Press* comes out three times weekly and the *Journal* comes out once a day.

It's real hot, and I'm starting to perspire, both because of the weather and I'm kind of scared. What if Ned has changed his mind and refuses to see me? I look in my pocket mirror. I like to prepare myself for both the best and the worst.

I go into the building. There is a big, circular desk built into the wall and a woman sitting behind it.

"May I help you?"

"Yes, I'm here to see William Nedlon Carther."

She's probably thinking, *You're the last person he'd have an appointment with.*

She presses some buttons on a telephone. "Mr. Carther isn't answering. You'll have to wait."

"Can I go into his office and wait for him?"

"No, we don't allow that. Everything has to be cleared with security."

You'd think I wanted to get into Fort Knox.

After what seemed like an eternity she presses the buttons again. "You can go up now. He's on the fourth floor."

When I get to the fourth floor, I register and am cleared. Then I walk into a big room that sounds of computer printers, typewriters and phones ringing. I don't see him anywhere.

"Where is William Nedlon Carther's desk?" I ask a lady who looks like a receptionist.

"He's stepped away," she tells me. "Who are you, anyway?"

"My name is Chris. I have an appointment with him."

"Oh, that girl he talked about from the restaurant."

A few minutes later, Mr. Carther and Wilber are walking toward me as if they were buddies from golf.

Chapter Eleven

What is going on here?'' I am beginning to think I'm on the verge of teenage senility or a nervous breakdown—maybe a combination of the two.

The three of us go into a private office. "There're a few things I neglected to tell you yesterday," Ned, a.k.a. William Nedlon Carther, tells me. "Because I didn't want to lay too much on you at one time. Wilber and I ran the Choo-Choo to do a probe on payoffs and graft in small businesses. After I worked undercover at a few small establishments I thought we'd set up our own operation with Wilber's help."

"But what about all the people who worked

there?'' I ask Wilber. "What's happening to them now that you closed it down?''

"They can all work for me when I go back into business. When my dad passed away, I inherited some money. I always wanted to go into the restaurant business. I used to work at the *Burlington Times* with Ned. When Ned came home last Christmas, I was thinking seriously of trying something else besides newspaper work. It gave Ned a brain wave. We thought it would be a good chance for me to learn the restaurant business, move to the big city and do a series together.''

"But nobody would send their cockroaches to eat there after they read those articles.''

"You're dead wrong,'' Ned answers. "Knowing the human animal, they'll come out of curiosity. Besides, Wilber will go under another name next time, and I'll make sure we review his place—fairly of course. The food was good there.''

Wilber laughs.

"Out of curiosity,'' I ask, "will you be hiring Roger?''

"I don't think so,'' Wilber shakes his head. "I wasn't too thrilled with his milk shake tactics. I suppose I led him to believe he didn't need to care. And even though I don't have any proof, I think he may have been part of a conspiracy to steal veal cutlets, hot dogs and tuna.''

I don't say anything.

Wilber looks at me. "Fifty pounds of meat isn't a felony. I just like to know that's all."

I nod my head yes. "I wonder how he got it out of there anyway."

"Well, things like that happen in business," Wilber says. "If you'd like to come back and work for me, you can."

"Thanks but no thanks. I've got to start back to school in a few weeks."

"I thought you did a great job," Wilber answers. "I'll have to admit I almost fell over when all that liquor was thrown out. I had already dumped it. It fried me out when I saw more bottles gone."

"Where was Ned that morning anyway?" I ask him.

"I had something to do over here at the *Journal* office," Ned answers. "It was almost time to shelve the Choo-Choo project anyway. I was afraid somebody might recognize me soon and I was afraid you'd be one of the somebodies."

We all laugh.

"I guess I better get back to my place. They're rewiring today," Wilber says. "Nice seeing you again, Chris." He hands me an envelope.

"This isn't a payoff, is it?" I tease Wilber.

"No, of course not. You never picked up your final check."

"Nice seeing you, Wilber, and thanks."

He picks up his expensive-looking sport coat and walks out.

"I guess you have something for me." Ned smiles and glances at my folder.

I hand it to him. He opens it and reads it over while my stomach plays hoptoad. I can already imagine him making confetti out of it. With all the electric typewriters and computers drumming outside this room, I hardly think anything typed on an ancient Smith Corona has a chance.

"This is a good counterview of the situation. I'll give it to the editor and see to it that it's printed as a sidebar the day we use your interview. Now about that interview..."

The second I leave the *Journal* I run over to city hall to locate Lou. A few other kids from the project are sitting by a desk stamping sheets of paper and putting them in envelopes.

"Hey, what's up?" Lou says when he sees me.

"Plenty." I tell him the whole story. "I wasn't so crazy now, was I?"

Lou looks at me and chews the end of his pencil. "I never thought you were nuts or I wouldn't have followed that guy for you or looked up the place in the tax bills. You must be thinking about another guy."

"I guess I was." My mind focuses on Roger. "And does the *Youth Observer* use free-lancers? Maybe we could do that corruption article together."

"Well, Anne Marie is the editor. The policy is high school students only." He laughs. "Before you talk to her, I have a confession to make."

"Is it juicy?"

"Not really. Things didn't work out so well with Anne Marie. Her boyfriend came back from Europe." Lou looks at me with those big brown eyes, the ones that used to seduce me into sharing my best crayons with him. "I was wondering if you'd go with me to the mock ball at the country club. It's this Saturday."

Considering I have not had one date all summer, except that dismal party I went to with Roger, I accept graciously. With Lou there's no hiding emotions. I throw my arms around him. "Should I wear a full-length red or black-and-white?"

"How about back-and-white? It could be reminiscent of your mix-up with the newspaper."

A few days later the story with my interview breaks in the paper and I hear from Roger.

"You weren't so far off for a sixteen-year-old. I'm sorry I got so mad at you."

"How did you get my number?"

"From your cousin. I was wondering if you'd like to go out Saturday. One of my friends is having a party."

"Sorry, but I have other plans."

"See you around," he says. "I guess I'll have to ask somebody else."

Not that stealing meat is the crime of the century. Even if he hadn't ripped it off, I can't get thrilled with somebody who takes me to a place called The Greasy Grind and a dismal party for a date. I'd rather date somebody who takes life a little more seriously. In fact, I'd rather not slide by in life anymore.

* * * * *

QUANTITY	BOOK #	ISBN #	TITLE	AUTHOR	PRICE
☐	1	98001-9	Does Your Nose Get in the Way, Too?	Arlene Erlbach	$2.25
☐	2	98002-7	Lou Dunlop: Private Eye	Glen Ebisch	$2.25
☐	3	98003-5	Toughing it Out	Joan Oppenheimer	$2.25
☐	4	98004-0	Lou Dunlop: Cliffhanger	Glen Ebisch	$2.25
☐	5	98005-7	Guys, Dating and Other Disasters	Arlene Erlbach	$2.25
☐	6	98006-5	All Our Yesterdays	Stuart Buchan	$2.25
☐	7	98007-8	Sylvia Smith-Smith	Peter Nelson	$2.25
☐	8	98008-6	The Gifting	Ann Gabhart	$2.25
☐	9	98009-4	Bigger is Better	Sheila Schwartz	$2.25
☐	10	98010-8	The Eye of the Storm	Susan Dodson	$2.25
☐	11	98011-6	Shock Effect	Glen Ebisch	$2.25
☐	12	98012-4	Kaleidoscope	Candice Ransom	$2.25
☐	13	98013-2	A Kindred Spirit	Ann Gabhart	$2.25
☐	14	98014-0	The Right Moves	M. K. Kauffman	$2.25
☐	15	98015-9	Lighten Up, Jennifer	Kathlyn Lampi	$2.25
☐	16	98016-7	Red Rover, Red Rover	Joan Hess	$2.25
☐	17	98017-5	Even Pretty Girls Cry at Night	Merrill Joan Gerber	$2.25
☐	18	98018-3	Angel in the Snow	Glen Ebisch	$2.25
☐	19	98019-1	The Haunting Possibility	Susan Fletcher	$2.25
☐	20	98020-5	Dropout Blues	Arlene Erlbach	$2.25

Your Order Total $ _____

☐ (Minimum 2 Book Order)

Add Appropriate Sales Tax $ _____

Postage and Handling _____ .75

I Enclose _____

Name _____

Address _____

City _____

State/Prov. _____ Zip/Postal Code _____

BOCR-2